Christmas Deadline

by

Pam Binder

Christmas Deadline

Cover Art by *Abigail Owen*

The Wild Rose Press, Inc.
PO Box 708
Adams Basin, NY 14410-0708
Visit us at www.thewildrosepress.com

Publishing History
First Champagne Rose Edition, 2020
Trade Paperback ISBN 978-1-5092-3299-4
Digital ISBN 978-1-5092-3300-7

Published in the United States of America

As the sleigh glided around a bend, Holly leaned her head on Noel's shoulder, and he bent over to place a kiss on her forehead. The gesture felt intimate and natural as he focused on the deserted road ahead that meandered under a canopy of trees.

Their homes were still separated by an ocean and thousands of miles, but they were together now. She didn't want to dwell on the future anymore. She wanted to live in the present and build a life from that point forward. And she hoped his kiss promised that he wanted her as much as she wanted him.

Feeling bold, she rested her gloved hand on his thigh and felt his muscles flex from her touch. His response sent a quiver of pleasure racing through her body as though lightning had electrified the air.

The horses picked up speed, and Noel chuckled softly, then reined them back down to a walk. "Whoa, boys." He chuckled again and slid a sidelong glance toward Holly. "We'll be home soon."

Home.

Under the velvet night's ceiling of stars, the word took on a new meaning for Holly. Noel had said it as though it was *their* home. The word conjured a future together. A future that included days filled with heart-pounding adventures, and nights devoted to making love, interlaced with cherished moments of coffee and conversation by the fireplace.

"Holly…" He turned toward her, and his voice was as molten as his gaze. "I want to kiss you."

He was asking for more than a kiss, and she knew she longed for that as well.

Time shifted, listening for her answer.

Praise for Pam Binder

"Pam Binder gracefully weaves elements of humor and romantic tension."

~*~

Awards
2018 Romantic Times
Pioneers of Romance Fiction Award

Dedication

To my daughter, Kelli Irene

Chapter One

Last night the rain and wind in Derby, England had been merciless, as though testing Noel Atteberry's resolve to protect Mistletoe Manor, his lands, and his animals. Early this morning the relentless wind had found the stable's weakness and a section of the roof had collapsed, panicking the horses inside. He'd spent the better part of the day rounding up the strays. The colt stranded in the fast-moving stream was the last. The storm's timing couldn't have been worse. Noel was on a book deadline, and he and his coauthor had reached a creative impasse.

A veil of mist the shade of chimney smoke on Christmas morning had blurred the stream and surrounding forest, which made finding the missing colt a challenge. It hadn't helped that the rain washed out the animal's tracks almost as fast as they were made. Noel had caught a lucky break when he'd heard the colt's cry of panic.

A snow-white colt stood in the middle of the stream, wide-eyed and frozen in place. Noel called out, but the frightened animal backed out into deeper waters.

"Bollocks," Noel said under his breath as he waded out into the ice-cold water. He'd helped with the colt's birthing but had yet to give the animal a name.

Here he was, supposedly this bestselling thriller

writer, and he couldn't come up with a name for the colt. It shouldn't surprise him. He had trouble naming the characters in his books. It wasn't a simple matter of knowing the meaning of a name; the name had to connect to the story and evoke an emotional response. And last but not least, the name had to fit the character.

Sometimes he had it right on the first try. Most often he changed the names midstream. In some instances, he'd write a scene between him and his characters and ask them straight out if they liked their names, which always made him wonder: if people in real life could change their names, would they?

His mother's favorite time of the year had been the Christmas season, and that's why she had named him Noel. Coincidentally, his coauthor was romance writer Holly Lane. He hadn't figured out yet if the name suited her. Her author bio sounded distant and formal, nothing like the lighthearted and friendly tone in her novels and emails. It was their publisher's idea to pair them for a current novel, which had gone well until they'd started writing the last third of the story.

He and Holly couldn't agree on how to end the novel, and that was a big problem. If they missed the deadline to turn it in on Christmas Eve, they'd have to return the advance.

He had another deadline looming that was even more ominous. He had to pay back a loan or lose his home.

The colt nickered as Noel approached. He reached out his hand. "Easy, boy. I agree, the water is freezing, and it's scary out here alone. Let's get you out of here and back into a nice warm barn. Your mother will be happy to see you. That storm last night was a real bugger. I don't blame you for running away. I've had the same thoughts lately. Be thankful you don't have deadlines."

The colt nudged Noel's shoulder playfully. "Did you like the name Deadline?" Noel nodded. "It's yours. Maybe using it as a name instead of a curse word will help turn my luck around."

He led the colt to shore and down the path that led back to the estate. "I'll make sure you have a safe place tonight, even if it's in my room." He chuckled. "Not so sure that would be an improvement, though. The roof on the manor is not that much better than the stable's. We're in a real pickle, young one. We're land rich and cash poor, as the saying goes."

The colt nickered as though in response, and Noel chuckled again.

"If you don't like the name Deadline, how about Storm?"

The colt slid Noel a glance.

Noel laughed outright. "You're right. Every time you'd hear that name you would remember this day. I'll keep working on it."

Chapter Two

Holly Lane stormed through the brass-and-gold double doors of the National Trust and Loan Bank, clutching an envelope. She was the bank's first customer. The piped-in song, "It's Going to Be a White Christmas," which usually put her in the holiday mood, did nothing to lift her spirits. She was on a mission.

This was only the second time she'd stepped foot in here, and it still reminded her more of a museum than a place of business, with its white marble floors, gray granite counters, and mahogany desks and woodwork. A twenty-foot, white, artificial Christmas tree decorated with gold ornaments completed the impression. Her boyfriend was the son of the bank's owners, and they liked their holiday decorations understated. Her mother called the look cold and impersonal.

"May I help you?" said a young woman in a tailored suit, who rushed over to greet her. The woman had chin-length black hair and a smile as artificial as the Christmas tree.

"My name is Holly Lane," she said with an edge to her voice, "and I have an appointment with Derek Williams."

The woman's expression froze and then broke into a warm smile that transformed her appearance as she reached for Holly's hand. "You're *the* Holly Lane? Omigosh. Mr. Williams didn't mention your name when he told me he had an appointment this morning. My name's Audrey, and I'm a big fan. I've read all your books: the Irish Love Poem series, Matchmaker Café series, and the Time Is an Illusion series. I'm looking forward to reading your first book in the Love's Temptation series you're coauthoring with Noel Atteberry. I heard the title is *Love Is Lost*. Do you know when it will be released?"

Holly flinched and focused on adjusting her messenger-style handbag across her shoulder. She wished she knew. She and Noel disagreed on how the book should end. She wanted the last chapter to end with the couple kissing and a happily-ever-after plotline. Noel agreed to the kissing part but wanted the couple to die in a fiery car crash.

To say that she and Noel were at a crossroads was an understatement. But if they didn't turn in the finished story by deadline, they would not only lose the final contract payment but would have to return their advance, too. However, the only thing she said to the young woman was, "We hope to turn in the finished manuscript to our editors over the holidays."

"Audrey, that will be all. I can take it from here," interrupted a tall man with a trimmed beard and dark suit. It was Derek. She'd told him she hated his beard. It was the one area where she and his father agreed. "That will be all, Audrey," Derek repeated.

Derek gave her a slight bow, taking Holly's elbow as he pulled her away from Audrey and headed in the direction of his office. When she'd first met him, she'd rationalized that his behavior toward those he worked with was professional, not patronizing. She also tried not to mind that he treated her like a client at the bank.

The heroes in her novels would have given their heroine a kiss and been nicer to Audrey.

Holding onto his annoyingly professional demeanor, Derek opened the door to a corner office bigger than her apartment and walked in first. Strike two. A gentleman would have let her go in first.

But even though her apartment was small, she missed it. She'd given it up when her stepfather had his heart attack. She'd moved back in with her parents to help her mother with his recovery after open-heart surgery, but one month had turned into three years.

Her parents' bills had been stacking up for months, and Holly suspected there wasn't enough money to go around. She knew things were tight and had offered to help. Her parents had refused. They had always been frugal and had saved for retirement. But with the rising medical costs, there never seemed to be enough. And now they might lose their home.

Derek shut the door to his office. He'd had his interior designer line the shelves with his law books and purchase first editions of Hemingway, Faulkner, and Robert Louis Stevenson. He boasted to Holly that although he'd only read the Cliff's Notes in school, having first editions of these prominent men made him look literary. When she offered to give him some of her books, he'd laughed and asked if she were joking. He had an image to maintain. His clients wouldn't be impressed with romance books.

His comment stung.

He motioned for Holly to take a seat as he sat down behind his desk and straightened his pen on the smooth surface. "You mentioned this was urgent. Couldn't it wait until after work? I can make reservations at that

Italian restaurant you like. We haven't spent much time together lately. You're always under deadline. You no sooner finish one novel than you start working on another."

Derek was only half right. It was true she had been busy, but he worked late and was gone most weekends. There never seemed to be time for them to spend together. If she was honest, though, it hadn't bothered her as much as it should.

Usually, the transition from one book to the next was smooth. Except this time she was working with a coauthor. She and Noel had worked well together on the first part of the novel but couldn't seem to agree on anything for the ending. Their editors, who had proposed the collaboration in the first place, were not sympathetic and suggested Holly and Noel meet face to face. They'd tell the world it was for publicity, but the real reason was to make sure the book met the deadline.

All of their collaboration had been long distance. She lived in Seattle and Noel lived in Derby, England. Because she'd always wanted to visit England, she'd offered to meet in Derby and had booked her flight. Under the circumstances, however, there was no way she could leave. Which left things back in limbo.

Derek cleared his throat. "Plotting your next novel?"

Holly did a mental shake and glanced over at Derek. His lips were pressed together in a tight line. "Sorry, I was thinking about my trip to England."

He looked away, not meeting her gaze. "You know I'd love to go with you, but it's a busy time during the holidays. Besides, I don't know why you have to go anyway. You make a lot of money for your publisher.

Tell them no. Of late, you spend so much time online with Noel or writing that you are never available. And when we are together, you seem as though you're walking on eggshells."

This was not the first time Derek had made this comment. The truth was that she never felt relaxed around him. She never felt like herself. "Well, I'm not flying to England after all. After our business is concluded, I'm going to let my publisher know that Noel needs to come to Seattle."

"I'm glad to hear it. Do you want me to make a dinner reservation for this Saturday, then?" He cleared his throat. "It will give us more time to discuss what brought you here. I was able to fit you in, but I have an appointment in a few minutes. Are you finally in the market to buy a home? Was that your emergency? We here at National Trust and Loan would be happy to assist you."

Holly glanced toward Derek as he straightened another pen on his desk so it was parallel to the one he'd straightened a few minutes ago. He was speaking to her with the professional tone he used on clients. He then moved the picture of his Labradoodle a fraction of an inch to the left. He was nervous. His OCD only rose to this level when he was avoiding something. They'd been dating for about four months and lately didn't seem to have time to fit each other into their schedules. She'd written this scene before and knew how it ended. If he wanted to break up, she was about to make it easier for him.

She shoved the crumpled envelope she held toward him and got straight to the point. "Someone in your bank sent my parents a foreclosure notice."

His expression faltered as though she'd thrown cold water on him. He opened the envelope. "Mr. and Mrs. Donnelly? I wasn't aware they were your parents." As though that information would somehow appease her. He looked up from the notice and forced a smile. "Perhaps if I'd known…"

Her blood began to boil. "What you're saying is that you might have spared my parents, but you and your bank would have coldheartedly foreclosed on another family over the holidays. How could you be so heartless? Have you not seen the zillion movies based on the character Scrooge?"

"Let me explain…"

She shook away his offer of explanation with a shake of her head. "I know what you're going to say because I've heard it from you before. You'll tell me that it's just business, nothing personal. Maybe that's what's wrong. How could it not be personal? You and your bank are kicking people out of their homes! And regarding my parents, you never wanted to meet them, remember?" She took in a deep breath to calm down. "My mother remarried when I was barely a year old." Holly leaned forward, resting her hands on his polished desk. "And who they are should not be the point. You're foreclosing on good people during the Christmas season. Did you offer to help them refinance?"

The color on his face rose as he smoothed his beard with his hand, eyeing the smudges her hands had left on his desk. He was as agitated as she was. "That is no longer an option," he said with an edge.

She leaned back against her chair and folded her arms across her chest. "How much?"

He sat up straighter. "I beg your pardon?"

"How much to pay off the loan?"

"You can't be serious. Your parents refinanced to help send you and your three brothers to college. The balance would wipe out your savings."

She reached into her purse and withdrew her checkbook. "Check or cash, or can you transfer the money directly from my account?"

Chapter Three

Later that day, Holly stared at her blank computer screen in her room over her parents' garage. Next to her was the folder containing the signed papers from the bank. She'd paid off her parents' mortgage. Their home was safe from foreclosure, but what else had her parents kept from her?

She concentrated on repositioning a Christmas tree sticker her mother had pasted on her computer screen. There was also a new Santa Claus pillow on her bed, a string of lights around her window, and a few more ornaments on the tabletop fir tree in the corner.

While Holly was away that morning, her mother had added more decorations to her room. Holly didn't mind, or at least she'd gotten used to her mother's obsession with decorating every inch of the house. It made her mother happy, and that was a good thing. How was she going to tell her mother she'd paid off the mortgage? Would she be upset?

When Holly had moved in three years ago to help her parents after her stepfather's heart attack and surgery, her mother rarely had smiled. She had been worried her husband wouldn't make it. Now laughter was back in the house.

Since the move, Holly had added a bed, a desk, a bookshelf, and a few odds and ends, keeping the rest in storage. After all, the move was supposed to have been temporary. She now had her doubts.

She looked over again at the blank computer screen. Well, not exactly blank. She'd written the words, "How will this story end?"

The characters in her novel weren't the only ones in limbo. She'd depleted her savings, was living with her parents, and if she and Noel couldn't agree on an ending, she'd have to figure out a way to repay the advance.

She moved from her desk to the bed, moving her suitcase to the center as she unzipped it and pulled out a Christmas-red wool sweater. She emailed Noel about her change in plans and cancelled her flight. Her parents were her first priority.

Holly set the sweater aside and reached in to retrieve a mesh square bag that held her silk nightgown and underthings. She'd never traveled to Europe and at her mother's encouragement had bought all new clothes, including the strapless little black dress her mother insisted she buy. It all seemed frivolous now.

She heard the door open and turned. The smell of gingerbread wafted into Holly's room as her mother stood on the threshold. Confusion etched her features as she scanned the open suitcase on her way to the tabletop tree.

Her mother's short, white hair curled around her round, rosy-pink face. Holly couldn't remember a time when her mother wasn't baking or cooking or wearing an apron she'd quilted from scraps of bright print fabric. She was the kind of person who gave you a hug, even if she was meeting you for the first time.

Her mother added a candy-cane-shaped ornament to the tree and stepped back. "Can you believe it? I only paid twenty-five cents for it, and I'm pretty sure it's handblown glass. I bought it at our church garage sale last Sunday."

"It's beautiful," Holly said. "I like the antique ornaments you find at garage sales the best. You have a great eye. There's a huge flea market next weekend. We should go."

Her mother's eyebrows pinched together as she headed to Holly's bed. "You'll still be in England. There will be others. Why did you unpack your lovely new sweater?" Her mother reached for the sweater on the bed. "Did you change your mind about bringing it? London is cold and damp this time of year."

Holly took the sweater from her mother. "How do you know it's cold and damp there? You and Dad have never traveled outside of Winter Valley, Washington."

"We travel. We went to your college graduation in Eastern Washington." Her mother snatched the sweater back and grinned as she placed it on the suitcase. "Besides, the reason I know so much about England is I read historical novels written by my famous daughter. By the way, when are you going to finish that beautiful romance historical you started a few years back?"

Holly sat down next to her suitcase. "My publisher only wants contemporary novels these days." She paused. "Mom, there's something we need to discuss."

Her mother sat down next to her on the bed. "What has happened? Did you finally come to your senses and break up with Derwood?"

"His name is Derek, Mom, and yes, we did break up. I visited his bank this morning, and we called it off. He didn't say so, but I think he's seeing someone else."

Her mother reached over to squeeze her hand. "I'm

so sorry. Are you okay?"

"More than okay, actually. I'm relieved. I should have listened to you when you said you didn't like him, even though the two of you never met."

"That's not true. I met him."

Holly looked up. "When?"

Her mother fingered the luggage tag on Holly's suitcase. "John and I visited the bank a short time ago. Your boyfriend was very rude and made John so upset...but that's not the reason. Whenever you talked about him your voice would sound shrill, as though you were on the verge of screaming."

Holly joined her mom on the bed and gave her a hug. "You know me better than I know myself."

Her mother laid her hands in her lap, studying them as though they held an answer. "Are you going to tell me why you are unpacking?"

"I'm not going to England."

"You have to go. What about the novel you're writing with that nice young man, Noel Atteberry?"

"Mother, you've never met Noel."

"True, but you talk about him all the time and light up like a Christmas tree when you mention his name. What about the deadline?"

Holly stood slowly and crossed over to her desk and the folder containing the mortgage papers. "I'll figure something out. Maybe Noel will come to Seattle."

"He can't," her mother said firmly. "I want you to go. This trip will be good for you. I can feel it."

"Mom. I have to stay here with you and Dad. I found out how bad things are for you financially, and I can't leave until it's all sorted out. I took care of the most pressing issue this morning." Holly handed her mother the document that verified her parents' mortgage had been paid in full. "I paid your mortgage. You're not going to lose your home."

Her mother unfolded the paper, shaking her head slowly. "How did you know?" She wiped at her eyes with the edge of her apron. "Oh, baby, you shouldn't have done this. It was too much money. John and I would have figured something out. We'd already decided that this house is too big for us. We were looking at a small place closer to town."

"You love your home and your garden and your friends. You play the piano on Sunday for the church choir and oversee all their bake sales and garage sales, and you are in charge of the annual school auction. You can't move away, and now you don't have to. I know this is a big place. Too big for you to take care of by yourselves. That's another reason why I'm staying."

Her mother lifted her chin. "You will do no such thing. You are going to England. I will not allow you to throw away your career."

"I'm not throwing anything away. I can write here just as well as in England. I've already cancelled the flight and emailed Noel."

"And I'm not blind. The stark reality is that you aren't writing the way you used to. You're avoiding writing and doing a fabulous job at it, I might add. You told me your publisher wants you in Derby, England, and that it was not a suggestion. From the pictures Noel sent you, his estate is the perfect place for inspiration; it reminds me of the manor house from the Downton Abbey series we love so much. Think of it as research for your historical novel."

"I'm not going, and that's final."

Her mother folded her arms across her waist. "You *are* going. You are not the only stubborn person in this family."

Chapter Four

Holly yawned as she went downstairs in search of coffee or a strong cup of tea. Either would work. She needed something to jolt her out of her funk. It was early and dark outside, and yet she heard voices. Her parents always had been early risers, and she welcomed the company.

She'd tried to write last night, but the only thing she'd accomplished had been making space in the room for another bookshelf and falling asleep at her desk. She'd kept most of her books and furniture in storage when she'd moved in to help her parents. Now that she was planning to stay, she'd need a few things.

She stretched as she reached the bottom step and turned down the hallway into the kitchen.

The kitchen was the heart of the house and spread into a great room with a stone fireplace. Along the length of that room was a bank of windows overlooking a porch and a vegetable garden. A long trestle table her brother Simon had made divided the great room from the kitchen. This was the place where many of her favorite memories had occurred. It was in this kitchen where her family had made their major decisions. It was where she'd cried when she hadn't been asked to the prom and had been comforted by her mother. It was also where she'd filled out college applications, and where she had written her first novel.

This morning, turkey bacon sizzled on the stove. Her mother added sliced strawberries and blueberries to a bowl of cut pineapple and melon and set the fruit bowl on the table beside a plate of freshly baked scones.

Next to her mother stood her stepfather. His white beard was neatly trimmed, and he looked slimmer, a clear indication he was following his doctor's orders to exercise and watch his diet. He reached into the bowl for a strawberry. Her mother slapped his hand away playfully, telling him to wait. He responded by kissing her on the nose and received a broad smile as her face flushed to a rosy glow.

He turned toward Holly with a smile. "I'm glad you're here. Your mother was about to wake you. You'll be leaving in about an hour for the airport."

She was going to say her mother must have forgotten to tell him she wasn't going to England, when two of her three brothers entered from the back porch. She was the youngest in the family, but her brothers had never called her the baby, or a princess, which made her love them more.

Simon, the eldest, filled the doorway with his height and broad shoulders. He had taken over their father's lumber mill and looked every inch a lumberman with his faded jeans, red-plaid flannel shirt, and bushy red beard. Jasper, the youngest of her three brothers, entered on Simon's heels, clean shaven and wearing his red hair shoulder length, dressed in jeans and a T-shirt despite the chill in the air. Jasper had been considered the wildest of the bunch and only recently had returned from what he called his "misadventures." He'd been welcomed back as though no time had passed. Holly loved that about her family. No one was ever left behind or forgotten.

Then it hit her like the roof had fallen on her head. Simon and Jasper only visited their parents on the weekends. Holly crossed her arms over her chest. "What's going on?"

Her mother placed a platter of bacon and scrambled eggs in the center of the table and motioned for her sons to sit down. "I told you last night. You are going. Your plane leaves in six hours, so I made you a nice breakfast. I made scones but didn't have time to make clotted cream. No worries, there will be plenty where you are going. Oh, almost forgot. Simon offered to take you to the airport."

"Mother, we discussed this last night. It's all settled. I cancelled my flight and emailed Noel. I'm worried about you and Dad. Did you tell Simon and Jasper about the house? I'm sure if they knew they'd agree that you need me to stay."

Her mother wiped her hands on her apron. "John and I agreed that we shouldn't have kept secrets from our children. We called everyone last night and told them what you'd done."

Simon pulled up a chair at the table, sat, and shook his head as he reached for the bacon. "Holly, I wish you had called me. You didn't have to pay off the loan by yourself. All of us could have helped."

She put her hands on her hips. "Wait a second. Now I'm the bad guy?"

Simon laughed and winked at his mother. "I told you she'd react that way. No, what you did was awesome. I am so proud of you, but what I meant was that we're a family. One for all and all for one: the family motto. You're not alone. Our parents were there for us when we needed them, and now we can all pitch in to help them. I talked with Patrick and his wife last night. Although they are preparing for the arrival of their baby in a couple of weeks, they agreed to stop by every few days. My house is a short distance from here, and Jasper has sublet his apartment in town and will be staying here while you are away. Mom has wanted to introduce him to someone who sings in the choir at church. Everything is in place. You don't have to worry."

"I don't need Mom to find me a woman," Jasper protested, scooping eggs onto his toast.

Her mother handed Jasper a napkin. "You don't need help finding a woman. You need help finding a wife."

Jasper groaned and dropped his head into his hands, while his mother chuckled softly and cuffed him lightly on the shoulder.

Holly's mother then turned her attention to her son Simon and wagged her finger at him. "And don't you think I have forgotten about you, *Mister I-do-not-need-anyone*."

"It sounds like you have everything worked out," Holly said. "Except I already cancelled my flight and emailed my regrets to Noel," she repeated.

"Patrick took care of the flight," Simon said. "And because he is a commercial airline pilot, he was able to book your flight using his family-and-friends discount, and Mom emailed Noel."

"Mom, how do you know Noel?"

Her mother paused to offer Simon, Holly, and her husband more eggs. When they declined, she scooped the last of the eggs onto Jasper's plate. "Technically, I didn't contact Noel directly. I found his telephone number in your contact file and called his house. I talked to a nice older gentleman named Jarvis, who works for Noel. Jarvis assured me that Noel will pick you up at the airport when you arrive in London. Jarvis also told me to tell you that Noel is freakishly tall. Those were Jarvis' exact words."

Holly looked around the room. She was surrounded. It was like her first day of kindergarten all over again. The night before, she had refused to go to school. She had been shy and worried she wouldn't make any friends. Her mother had made a few phone calls. Patrick and Jasper drove all night from the colleges they were attending and joined Simon at the kitchen table when she had come down for breakfast. They agreed they would sit in her classes with her until she felt comfortable.

They'd all followed through on their promise. She'd been embarrassed until the kids told her how cool it was that her brothers had come to school with her. She'd realized that even the most outgoing person appreciated the support of family.

"I'm not going to win this, am I?"

Everyone shook their heads.

Chapter Five

The next morning, the weather had improved. Noel wasn't fooled, however. Mother Nature was just catching her breath, which meant he needed to prepare. He'd used the last of his advance to hire construction workers to repair the damage to the stables and ordered enough food supplies in case the creek rose again and washed out the roads. Last night he'd returned the colt to his anxious mother, and this morning he'd checked on them first thing. He'd even tried out a few more names on the colt, but the animal didn't seem impressed.

Noel hauled a bale of hay into the barn and then walked back toward the truck for another. He'd given up writing after he received Holly's email, which cited family issues as the reason she couldn't travel here so they could try to finish their novel. He understood completely. Families came first, which was the reason he had to stay in Derby. He had to look after his father.

It didn't surprise him that she put family before work, and it fit into the image he had of her through her writing. If they ever talked about author bios, he might suggest she revise hers. On the other hand, maybe the tone was deliberate, like the one he'd constructed for himself. Her email suggested they talk on the phone to work out the ending scenes. The idea was sound but strange. In all the time they'd been working together, they'd never talked. All their communication had been by emails. To use the phone, they'd have to deal with the eight-hour time difference. She might have a problem with that, but he wasn't sleeping much these days anyway, so it shouldn't be an issue.

Noel hefted a bale onto his shoulder, then pulled up short when he saw his father coming toward him from the manor. His father looked every inch a country gentleman in his tweed jacket, wool trousers, and cap. Noel remembered a time when he'd looked up to his father. That seemed like a lifetime ago. An unexpected twinge of regret shot through him. He gritted his teeth against the emotion. When it came to his father, he had to remain strong.

"Father, you should be in bed. The doctor said the damp air is not good for your arthritis."

His father waved away Noel's comment. "Why do you insist on doing manual labor?" his father said. "I don't understand why you dismissed everyone."

His father's comment caught him off guard, even though he'd thought by now there wasn't anything his father could do that would surprise him. Noel had had to let the majority of those who helped run the estate go two years ago. Had his father forgotten? Or was he trying to avoid the truth? Either way, it wasn't a good sign.

They were up to their eyeballs in debt because of his father's gambling.

Noel headed toward the barn, saying over his shoulder, "I didn't let everyone go. I was able to keep Jarvis and Clara on."

His father blocked his path. "No need to sugarcoat it. I know things are tight."

If things were only "tight" as his father put it, Noel might not be as worried. But as much as he wanted to rail at his father, he held back. It was true his father had caused their problems with his spending habits, but the man was also ill. His heart softened. This was his father. "When the final payment comes through on this new book, and if we cut corners, we might be able to make it through."

"A lot of ifs and whens, son. You attended Cambridge and are a bestselling author of thrillers and mysteries. Why are you writing romances?"

Noel set the bale of hay down. Of late, it was becoming increasingly difficult to keep the resentment toward his father out of his voice, and he hated that it was there in the first place. Once upon a time they'd had a great relationship. "Rubbish. We've had this conversation before. My editor wants to expand my reader base, and so she paired me with a romance writer. I bring the action. Holly brings the romance."

His father shook his head and sighed. "I know the real reason was the big advance. You take a lot on your shoulders, son."

A rooster called out in the yard and another answered as the sun rose higher over the horizon. His father's expression slipped from the confident country gentlemen to that of a man who'd lost his way. Noel had heard his friends say that as a parent aged there was a role reversal. The parent became the child and the child the parent. He'd expected it might happen, but not this soon. But since it had, he once more strengthened his resolve. He loved his father but would not be drawn in again by false promises.

"We are in this together, Father. Now, if you'll

excuse me, the horses are hungry, and I still haven't mended the fence out back. Oh, and Holly Lane cancelled. She's not coming after all."

"That's a shame. I was looking forward to meeting her. I even bought one of her novels at the bookstore in town. Haven't read it, though. I was never into all that lovey-dovey stuff like your mother. Happy endings are a myth."

His father's spin on romance hadn't always been this jaded. But Noel figured that losing his wife when she was still so young was no doubt the cause.

"Mable sold you a romance novel?" he said in an attempt to change the subject away from his mother.

"You talk about Holly Lane all the time, and Mable said she was her favorite." He paused. "Next to you, of course."

Mable had been like a mother to him when his mother died from cancer and his father had reacted by spending money they didn't have. She was the one who had alerted Noel to his father's gambling. If not for Mable, Noel wouldn't have taken over the finances. But after all the cuts and restructuring, the truth was that Noel might simply have delayed the inevitable. Too much damage had already been done.

Noel nodded. "Father, you should get back inside. I'm sure Clara has breakfast ready."

"There's something we need to discuss first. I've been thinking about our situation."

"You mean the situation you placed us in with your gambling?"

His father avoided Noel's gaze. "I'm better now. I'm going to get help."

"Hope so."

"As I started to say, the widow Lady Catherine Montgomery intends to pay us a visit. I heard in town that she is in the market for another husband. Didn't the two of you date at Cambridge? I know she regrets breaking your heart when she married Montgomery. Our estates border one another, and a marriage with Catherine would solve all our financial problems."

This wasn't the first time his father had brought his ex's name up in this context. He and Catherine had dated at Cambridge and even talked about marriage in some fabled distant future. The discussions and the relationship ended soon after graduation. Years later, he'd received an invitation to her wedding.

He'd attended the wedding. It would have been bad form if he hadn't; after all, they were going to be neighbors. Catherine was engaged to Lord Montgomery, who was the same age as Noel's father. It wasn't a secret that she wanted the title of Lady Catherine more than she wanted the man. Noel didn't judge. His own great-grandmother had come from America looking for a man with a title. She was the heiress to a fortune, and his great-grandfather had been in debt because of the money he had given to support the war effort.

The Montgomery wedding was a lavish affair, and Catherine made a beautiful bride. Noel had expected to feel jealous at seeing her marry. Instead, he was happy she was happy, and over the years they had become friends. He'd also attended her husband's funeral last year.

But marriage?

He was not getting married. At least the part in his author's bio that claimed he was a confirmed bachelor was true. Marriage was not for him.

Noel lifted the bale of hay onto his shoulder again. It was so like his father to take the easy road. "Marrying Catherine is out of the question. We will figure out another way."

As Noel turned to leave, his father reached for his arm. "Promise me you'll consider it."

****

A few hours later, Noel entered the manor from the back, into an earth-brown tiled entry his mother had nicknamed the mud room. When she realized her son was more interested in playing outside regardless of the climate, she ordered the room constructed and fitted with a bathroom, complete with a shower and shelves of towels and clean clothes.

His father had objected and reasoned that his own father would have frowned on any family member—with a title and a claim to the throne, however distant—entering the manor at the back like a servant was unthinkable.

His mother had won the argument, as she often did, and even though she was gone, Noel had insisted the mud room remain functional. In fact, he rarely entered by the main entrance. The mud room reminded him of his mother and the small battles she had won. His mother believed that it wasn't title or wealth that made the person, it was the generosity of their heart.

He pulled off his boots and then recognized the knock on the door leading into the rest of the manor. It was Jarvis. The man had been with Noel's family since his grandfather's time, and Noel considered him a friend.

"Come in, Jarvis. I'm decent."

White-haired, with a trimmed mustache and wearing a dark suit, Jarvis always looked like he could step comfortably into the Victorian era of Jane Austen's *Pride and Prejudice*. Jarvis' deep-throated chuckle always sounded to Noel like a bear—a human and friendly bear. "Yes, you are a decent chap, sir, in more ways than one."

"Thank you, but I fear you see only the good in everyone, old friend."

"I see clearly, despite the age in these old eyes. The wife and I saw what you did last night to save the animals. Your mother would have been proud."

Noel sat on the bench and peeled off his wet stockings, noting the holes in his boot socks. "My mother would have been right there beside me last night."

"That she would, sir, that she would. Begging your pardon, but that's not the only reason I'm here. Your editor called...again. She said she expects the new pages on or before Christmas Eve. If you don't mind my saying, sir, she sounded a bit like an Ebenezer Scrooge."

Noel leaned his head against the wall. "In her defense, she's been very patient. Is that all?"

"No, sir, not quite. Holly's mother contacted me to inform you that her daughter is coming after all. I told Holly's mother that you will be at the airport to meet her daughter when she arrives. I've written down the flight information for you. And Lady Montgomery is waiting for you in the drawing room."

Noel pushed to his feet. "Bloody hell."

"Indeed, sir, indeed."

Chapter Six

The drawing room was designed to capture as much of England's stingy light as possible, and in the manor's glory days, it had entertained the nobility. Banks of glass windows formed three walls that looked out onto the winter gardens. The solid wall where the room attached to the manor was decorated with a mural depicting the gardens at Windsor Castle. He didn't exactly dislike the room. He just never saw the point. Why create a room that was like the outdoors when all you had to do was walk outside and experience said outdoors?

Noel stood out of sight in the doorway. He'd showered and changed into clean clothes He'd joked with Jarvis that, instead of jeans and a sweater, perhaps he should wear the suit of arms standing in the entry like a medieval guard, explaining that his meetings with Catherine and her solicitor, Reginald Taylor, were like going into battle. Jarvis' only response was a twitch of his mustache.

In the center of the room, Lady Catherine Montgomery sat opposite his father, having tea and exchanging polite laughter and cautious smiles. For once, her solicitor was not present. Nonetheless, the formality pressed around Noel as he girded his loins, as the saying went, and entered.

"There he is," his father said, rising to greet his

son. "What are you wearing? Didn't Jarvis tell you we had a guest?"

Noel should have worn the suit of arms. "Jarvis told me."

Dressed in a navy-blue suit, Catherine rose as stiff and perfect as a porcelain doll, her chin-length straight blonde hair barely moving. "Lord Atteberry, I don't mind. In truth, he looks rather dashing in a rustic sort of way. Jarvis mentioned that Noel was up all night working to make sure all the animals were found. He is to be commended that he cares so much for his lands."

His father grumbled something incoherent and motioned for Noel to join them.

The chair, with its rosebud print and gilded wood, was about as comfortable as it looked. Catherine and his father talked nonstop about the importance of bloodlines and tradition as she poured him tea in a small, fragile-looking teacup. He forced it down. He'd never been a tea drinker, which Holly had pointed out to him was very un-English. Remembering their lighthearted exchange and his promise to give tea a try brought a smile to his face. Nevertheless, he liked his coffee black, and the stronger the better. The moment he could escape, he'd make a pot of coffee. It was going to be a long day.

With Holly coming, he'd need to look over the last chapter and maybe add another scene. He admitted he was both excited and anxious to see her in person. They'd never met, yet he felt he knew her better than any of the friends he'd known since he was a child. He supposed that happened when you corresponded with someone for over a year. Plus, there were her novels...

"Noel, didn't you hear Lady Catherine's generous

offer?"

Noel scrubbed his face with his hand. "I apologize. With everything else going on with the estate, my editor is on my case to finish my novel."

Catherine refilled his teacup, even though he hadn't asked. "I keep forgetting you write novels. After we're married, and with my infusion of cash into your estate, you'll have more time to spend with your writing hobby. I have many charities and interests in the arts as well, so we will make the perfect pair. I believe it's essential for married couples to have separate interests. Of course, I'll expect you to attend a few charity fundraisers from time to time, and I'll attend your book signings." She paused. "Do they still do book signings these days?"

"Not as often, but it does happen." Noel finished his lukewarm tea in one gulp. The quip about his writing being only a hobby didn't bother him. She'd always been more interested in fashion magazines and gossip columns than novels. He gave her a pass because he knew she was serious about her charities. She had money and position, and she used both to help others. What had his mind reeling was the offer of marriage. His father had mentioned the possibility, but Noel had considered it little more than wishful thinking on his father's part as an easy solution to their financial problems.

"Marriage?" he said, letting the word flow out on a breath. "Unless there is fine print in your husband's will that I'm not aware of, the conditions are clear. The loan he gave my father must be repaid in full, either in land or cash, exactly one year after the lord's death. The anniversary of his death is still a couple of weeks away.

You deserve more than what would amount to an arranged marriage. We both do."

Catherine reached over and put her hand over his. "Dear Noel. We are no longer children. The days of waiting for my prince charming to sweep me off my feet are long gone. You are a good man, and they are hard to find these days. I no longer want drama in my life. There is no fine print. The terms of the will are straightforward. But when we marry, your land will become mine and satisfy the conditions of the will. I want stability. I'm not asking for your decision today. All I ask is that you think it over."

"It's a good offer, son."

It was a good offer. So why did he feel as though he wanted to blow something up? He blamed Holly's romance novels and her insistence that everyone deserved a happily-ever-after ending. Bah, humbug.

Chapter Seven

Holly felt like she had been sleepwalking through endless lines. A line to disembark the plane when it landed at London's Heathrow Airport. A line to get her luggage. A line to go through customs, and a line that led out of the airport. The passageway leading outside opened into a wide area where people waited for those disembarking the planes. Friends and family greeted their loved ones, while others held up signs that varied from a person's name to the name of a tour or that of a cruise line.

She scanned the signs, looking for her name. Jarvis had told her mother that Noel was freakishly tall. Height was subjective. Her mother was five-three in heels: anyone over six feet would seem like a giant. Holly, on the other hand, took after her birthfather's side of the gene pool and was five-ten. This guy would have to be really tall to qualify as tall in her eyes.

Holly slowed her pace, again scanning the row of signs, again looking for her name. Men and women held up signs, many dressed professionally in suits or in clothes with the logos of their tour group or cruise line. But so far, she didn't see her name on any of the signs. Then she spotted a good-looking man who, although he wasn't holding a sign, not only met the "freakishly tall" criterion but also looked as though he was searching for someone.

But this was not just any attractive guy. This was a drop-dead gorgeous, heart-stopping, big-as-a-mountain type man. She'd always considered her brothers tall, but this guy was demigod tall. He wore a tweed jacket, with leather-patched sleeves, over a white shirt and jeans, and his face was weathered as though he worked outside or tamed winds on the high seas. He was the type of man she wrote about in her novels. He was the knight in the Middle Ages, a disinherited prince, a captain aboard a ship bound for the colonies.

She mentally shook herself. No, that wasn't quite right. The man standing before her was edgier, more recent history than medieval, with an untamed expression around the eyes.

Then she had it. He looked like someone who might live in the Wild West and right a wrong. Maybe a cowboy or someone who was part Native American with English or French ancestry. He could rope and ride and shoot a gun, maybe even a bow and arrow.

Her imagination drifted to the wilds of the volatile West after the Civil War. Her teachers had admonished her for daydreaming through her classes, and Derek had claimed she daydreamed during their conversations—a comment that unfortunately was often true.

But even knowing what was happening, she couldn't stop the flow, and the truth was that she didn't want to stop it. Her stories appeared like movies in her thoughts. Sometimes they were still-shots, and sometimes the whole scene played out, complete with dialogue, setting, and emotion. It was easier to live in an imaginary world where she could control the outcome and where she knew there would be a happily-ever-after.

The sights and sounds of the airport blurred as her story gained momentum. Holly allowed the images to expand and flow. She imagined that her heroine, Amber Rose, stood at a deserted train station in Montana...or maybe Wyoming. Originally, Holly had pitched an outline for a western with Amber as the heroine with only a vague idea of the plot and hero, but her editor said they no longer wanted historical novels from Holly, only contemporaries. Regardless, Holly couldn't forget Amber.

Holly couldn't shut down her imagination once it began to flow. What if Amber Rose had arrived at the train station in the late eighteen nineties? What if Amber had answered an ad in a Pennsylvania newspaper requesting a schoolteacher for a small western town? The ad had been written by the town's mayor, Douglas Greyeyes, who was an eligible bachelor and ridiculously handsome. A little cliché, but Holly would spice it up, add a few twists. It would be her first book with a Native American as a hero. What if her hero had been educated at Oxford, was a lawyer, owned the majority of the buildings in the town Amber was visiting?

"Holly Lane?"

Startled, she snapped back to the present and looked up, up, up into storm-gray eyes. Leaning back, she lost her balance. Her character had come to life. "Douglas Greyeyes?"

The man caught her before she fell. "No, it's Noel Atteberry. Who's Douglas?"

Chapter Eight

Holly sat on the passenger side of Noel's vintage forest-green Porsche as he drove toward a small village with ivy-covered brick buildings, wide sidewalks, and lamp posts decorated like Christmas candy canes. Noel drove on what he called the "proper side" of the car, while she attempted not to feel uncomfortable. It felt odd to sit on the side of the car where she would normally be driving. Along a narrow stretch of road, and without slowing, he made a sharp, hairpin turn, and then another.

She grabbed the door handle and pressed both feet on the floor as though she could slow down the car. Holly wanted to ask Noel if he had a death wish and would he please take it easy, but she wasn't sure he'd listen. How well did she really know him?

She hadn't said more than a few words to Noel since their first meeting, when she had called him Douglas Greyeyes. How embarrassing.

Noel had asked her about it, and she'd told him the truth. She'd been plotting a story and forgotten where she was. He'd nodded, saying he did that as well, and to her relief, dropped the subject. Thankfully, he hadn't asked why she'd called him Douglas Greyeyes or had almost swooned when he'd leveled his gaze in her direction.

Her face still felt flame red. True, Noel was good-looking, but so was Derek. In Noel's case, it was more than good looks. There was something about him. An old-world feel that made her knees go weak and her mind turn to mush. He had the confident look of a man who could lead armies on impossible quests and survive: Indiana Jones meets John Wick.

She resisted the impulse to fan her face. Her imagination wasn't helping. She leaned against the car door and the cool, rain-soaked air pushing against the glass. She needed to get a grip. This was her coauthor, and if she had any hope of making the deadline, she'd have to figure out a way to tamp down her libido.

Their editors had tasked them not only with completing the manuscript but adding more romance, and she hoped they could deliver.

They'd sped out of London and its snarl of traffic, so like every other major city, and onto a highway in the direction of Derby. Every few miles the remains of a castle tucked into a copse of trees reminded her that she wasn't in New York or Boston, where buildings were considered old if they reached the ripe old age of one or two hundred years. In Europe, that would be considered new construction. The castles in England dated back a thousand years or more. Perhaps being surrounded by places she'd only read about had messed with her mind and that was the reason she'd drooled over a perfect stranger.

"Get a grip," she said. Her breath fogged the window, and on impulse she drew the shape of a heart with her finger.

"Did you say something? Are you all right?" Noel asked.

Startled, she rubbed the image away with the palm

of her hand and nodded that she was fine, not trusting herself to speak. What was happening to her? She was not herself today.

Noel left the freeway and turned down a road that led to a postcard image of a small English village. Had she really said, "Get a grip," aloud?

She concentrated on drinking in the quaint shops with their painted doors and window boxes with trailing ivy and holly, fat with red berries. Everywhere she looked there were Christmas decorations. Wreaths hung from doors and windows, the outline of a tree with lights could be seen behind a house, and in the center of town was a decorated tree that stood about eight stories high. Her mother would love this place and head straight for the thrift shops.

Holly sat forward. "Stop. There's a bookstore."

"We're almost to Mistletoe Manor. I thought you would like to rest and have a bite to eat before visiting the town."

She shook her head. This was the perfect distraction—she needed a little retail therapy to clear her thoughts. The bookstore was a beacon of calm and normalcy, and right now it felt like she needed that as much as she needed to breathe. She loved everything about bookstores, and this one looked straight out of a Jane Austen novel. What was almost as intriguing was the tidy antique store next door. "Please stop," she said, daring to turn toward him. Her breath caught in her throat. She put her hand on the door. Had the man grown handsomer since the airport? She cleared her throat. "I can't wait." She said it like she had to take a restroom break.

"If you insist." He checked for oncoming traffic,

slowed the car and slid into a parking spot near the bookstore.

The moment the engine was turned off, Holly bolted from the car. A welcoming blast of rain-kissed air cooled her cheeks as she splashed through puddles on the sidewalk and headed toward the bookstore on the corner.

She opened the door and a bell chimed in greeting. Ten or so people were there, looking over shelves of books or venturing into what she now realized was a combination café and antique shop. Comfy chairs were grouped in the corners of the bookstore, while others were positioned around a fireplace. In front of the cozy fire, a white-haired woman dressed like Mother Goose read to a half dozen rosy-cheeked boys and girls a Christmas story about a boy who found a lost reindeer and returned him to the North Pole. The woman peered over her rhinestone reading glasses as Holly entered the store.

The storyteller's smile broadened. "Oh, my. Children we have an author paying us a visit. Welcome, Holly Lane."

Holly froze for a split second and then smiled. She hadn't expected to be recognized and was pleasantly surprised. A few of her titles had made it to Europe and had been translated into German, French, and Italian. Still, that didn't mean she was a household name. "I don't want to disturb you," Holly said. "I saw your bookstore and had to visit."

The woman's laugh reminded Holly of the musical chimes on the door. "Our little bookstore has that effect on people. And once inside, many also visit the café and antique shop for a cup of tea or homemade soup and bread." The woman gave a warm smile in return as the bell over the door chimed again. "Children, what a treat. We now have a second author. It's our own mystery writer, Noel Atteberry. Noel, why don't you come over and finish reading to the children while I introduce myself to Miss Lane."

"It would be my pleasure, Mable."

The children gave a roar of cheers as he strolled over to them, accepted the book Mable offered, and sat down. One of the children, a boy with a mop of red hair, handed him a book about pirates. "This is a good one too, Jonah," Noel said. "We'll read them both."

Holly watched the scene before her unfold. Noel was comfortable with the children, calling them by name, asking about their families and how they were doing in school. He had taken the book the storyteller handed him and settled in the chair she'd vacated as though reading to children was as natural to him as breathing. Her first reaction to him shifted and warmed into something she couldn't quite identify. There was more to him than she realized.

The woman Noel had called Mable weaved around the children, and when she reached Holly, she swept her into a welcoming hug. "I've always wanted to meet you. You're even lovelier than your author picture. What brings you to our little town?"

Holly moved farther away from the cluster of children so as not to disturb Noel's reading. She hesitated before speaking. How much should she share with Mable? It was common knowledge that she and Noel were working together, but not that they were struggling to complete the project. She'd keep within the boundaries of what she'd shared with her readers.

"I'm here to work on the last chapters of the book I'm coauthoring with Noel."

Mable lifted an eyebrow and turned toward Noel. He had pulled one of the children onto his lap and was letting the small child turn the pages while he read. The other children had scooted their chairs closer so they could hear better. "So you're the author he's been talking about. Interesting."

Holly's pulse quickened. "Noel has been talking about me?"

"Every time he visits my bookstore and café," Mable said and turned her back toward Noel as she lowered her voice. "He mentioned that the two of you can't decide on an ending, and he may have called you a hopeless romantic."

Holly shot Noel a glance and felt her blood rise. What exactly was wrong with being a hopeless romantic? As though he'd sensed her glare, he looked up from reading to the children. She narrowed her gaze. "Oh, he did, did he?"

Mable straightened, gathered a stack of children's books, and started arranging them in the bay window. "How long will you be staying in Derby?" The tone of her voice held a hint of laughter.

Holly recognized the change of subject tactic and helped Mable with the books. "I'm hoping not very long. Noel and I can't figure out a way for our hero and heroine to end up together, and his comment that he believes I'm a hopeless romantic shouldn't have come as a surprise. I believe in happily-ever-after, and he believes in endings. As a result, we each have our own version. Noel wants everything to end in an explosion, and I want them to get married."

"Indeed." Mable patted Holly's hand as she glanced in Noel's direction. "Is this the first book you've written with Noel?"

Holly sat on the edge of a chair. "Yes, and it was going well. Both of our editors loved the characters we developed, the plot, and the early chapters. The beginning and middle were smooth as silk. It was only when we neared the end that we hit a roadblock."

Mable pulled Holly to her feet and drew her toward a bay window by the front of the store that held a display of books. "You say that your characters can't seem to get together in the end?"

Holly shook her head. "I've never had this trouble before. It's as though I've lost my romance mojo. You said Noel called me a hopeless romantic. I'm not sure that's true anymore. It feels like I'm going through the motions. If I'm being honest, our characters shouldn't end up together. Noel and I never set it up that way. Our characters experienced the occasional kiss and a moment of passion now and again. There was even a romantic candlelight dinner, but then there was an explosion and the characters moved on to a car chase scene. Our characters treat each other more like coworkers than people in love. My editor even made that comment, and I assured her we had it under control. But I'm not so sure. Noel is experiencing the same issue. Our editors thought if we met in person, we might be able to collaborate our way out of our funk."

Mable reached for a book from the display case and laid it on the table. "Noel's novels are exciting and involve car chases, murder, and yes, explosions, and at times there is a hint of romance. Not enough to my liking, and I've told Noel that on more than one occasion. I understand now why your editors put the two of you together. He can help you increase the action scenes, and you can help him spice up the romance. Have you ever read one of Noel's books?"

Holly scanned the cover of the book Mable held; it had a one-word title written in blood red on a black background: *Shattered*. The few mysteries and thrillers she'd read of Noel's only flirted with the idea of a relationship. "I'm sure Noel and I will figure it out."

Mable returned the book to the shelf. "Well, I hope you stay with us over the holidays. Derby is magical this time of year. They say it's the perfect time to fall in love."

Holly glanced over at Noel and then wished she hadn't. As though he'd sensed her staring, he'd looked up at that exact instant and smiled over at her, even going so far as to wink.

Holly's face warmed as she cleared her throat. Mable was as subtle as a department store Santa Claus. "Do you have a restroom I could use?"

Mable nodded toward the back of the store. "Is everything all right?"

She nodded as she headed toward the restroom. She needed space to clear her head. No, everything was not all right. She was crushing on a man she'd just met. Worse yet, she feared she had lost her ability to write a romance ending that would bring tears of joy to her readers. If she didn't get control of the situation, and soon, the career she'd worked hard to build would crumble.

****

Noel finished reading the book about pirates, setting it aside and promising the children he'd return

43

soon. Reading to them was a highlight for him, but he could tell they were growing restless. The youngest had fallen asleep in his lap. He picked her up and handed her over to her mother as Mable came over.

"Children," Mable said, "I have some lovely hot cocoa and fresh baked cookies in the café. Your parents are waiting, and after your snack, you can help me pick out another book to read."

A roar of cheers reverberated round the children as they raced to the café and their waiting treats. As soon as they were out of earshot, Mable knelt down beside Noel.

"Okay, tell me what's going on before Holly Lane returns."

"I have no idea what you're talking about. Holly and I only work together."

Mable harrumphed. "Rubbish. That line might work with strangers, but I've known you all your life. I spent the last few minutes talking to Holly, and the glances the two of you exchanged could heat my bookstore for weeks. Holly mentioned something about a deadline and nonsense about the two of you not being able to write a satisfactory ending. You know exactly how you want this story to end."

"You're not talking about the novel, are you?"

Chapter Nine

Noel sped onto the road that led to Mistletoe Manor. Since visiting the bookstore, Holly seemed like a different person, as though someone had turned on a switch. She couldn't stop talking about how much she'd enjoyed meeting Mable and spending time in the bookstore. Holly asked him questions about his books and his process. Did he write in the mornings or afternoons? Did he ever scare himself with the type of plotlines he wrote about? How did he conduct his research? Did he ever base his characters on real people?

She seemed genuinely interested in his writing process. He then asked her the same questions. It felt good to talk to a fellow author. He had few opportunities. His life consisted of writing novels and maintaining the estate. On the rare occasion he participated in book tours, it was always as the lone author.

He glanced in her direction. Her face was pressed close to the passenger-side window, her eyes wide with curiosity, and her full lips parted. What would it be like to kiss her? Would her mouth taste as good as it looked?

"Is this your home?" she said. Her voice jolted him back to reality as she pointed to the manor house at the end of the long, tree-lined drive. When he nodded, she added, "It's beautiful. My mother was right when she compared it to Downton Abbey. It must have been wonderful to grow up surrounded by so much beauty."

He cleared his throat, trying to see his home through her eyes. All he saw was a dodgy roof that leaked and needed repairs, and potholes in the circular drive.

He tore his gaze away. "The estate has been in my family for over seven generations. In its glory days, kings and queens visited on their way to and from London."

Holly pressed her face against the car window. "You must have lived the life most people only dream." She rolled down her window and scooted closer to the door.

He slid a glance in her direction again as his car rolled to a stop. He had anticipated her response. It was people's first reaction to Mistletoe Manor. Usually, he went along with the charade, but with Holly he wanted to be honest. He parked the car, keeping his hands on the steering wheel. "Actually, it was a money pit from the moment the construction ended. The architect and builders did too good a job, and at one time it was considered the finest home in the area. As a result, everyone wanted to stay here. Over the centuries, it was a favorite retreat for the kings and queens of England. They said their staying here was a great honor—and they required my ancestors to house and feed everyone at their own expense. There could be two to three hundred people in the monarch's company, and it almost broke the bank, as they say. We had to sell off more and more lands to survive."

Her cheery expression clouded over as she reached

over and rested her hand on his sleeve. "That's awful." The pressure on his arm along with the kindness in her eyes almost undid him as she gifted him with a smile. It was the open, genuine smile he'd seen in a picture once where she had been reading her first and only children's book to a library filled with school-age children.

"That must have been so hard on your ancestors," she continued. "But it is a testament to them that they fought to keep Mistletoe Manor in the family. I want to know more. And despite the freeloading kings and queens, I still think it's cool that your home once was visited by nobility. If I ever write a historical again, I'll include that plotline. I'll bet if the walls could talk, they'd make me blush with the tales of affairs and scandals. Too bad no one kept a journal."

He grinned, sensing her attempt to lighten the mood as well as loving that she hadn't taken her hand away but had moved closer to him. "Ah, but a few of my industrious relatives did just that. It was rumored that they used what they learned to blackmail some of the nobles, who would then pay handsomely for my ancestors' silence. The only journal that survived, as far as we know, was named *Whispers on a Pillow*."

"You're kidding! That is so cool. It sounds like the perfect title for an erotic romance novel." She squeezed his arm gently. "Please tell me you still have it."

His eyebrows drew together. "You don't write that type of novel."

She laughed. "Just because I don't write erotic novels doesn't mean I don't read them. Where is it kept?" she pressed.

He let out his breath, keeping his eyes focused straight ahead. This was a side of her he hadn't expected. "The journal is kept in the library. I haven't read it in its entirety, but a friend of mine read a few lines to me and they were definitely X-rated."

Her eyes widened and a soft pink blush heightened on her skin. "Weren't you curious how the story ends?"

Jarvis tapped on the passenger's window, and for once Noel was relieved at the interruption. Over a winter holiday in college, Catherine was visiting and had read a few of the passages from the journal to him, and one thing had led to another. *Whispers on a Pillow* made *Fifty Shades of Grey* look tame in comparison. The last thing he wanted was to read the journal together with Holly.

Jarvis held an umbrella in one hand as he tapped again. "Is everything all right, sir?"

No, everything is not okay, Noel wanted to say. He couldn't stop thinking about the journal and Holly's kissable mouth.

This morning his life had been uncomplicated. That was, of course, before he'd picked up Holly from the airport. He'd seen her author picture, and they'd corresponded through emails for almost a year. What he hadn't anticipated was how attracted he'd be to her when he met her face to face. When she looked up into his eyes, it felt like he'd been hit with a bolt of lightning. She'd mistakenly called him Douglas, and for a split second he'd considered answering to that name.

When Jarvis repeated asking him if he were okay, Noel gave Jarvis the thumbs-up that everything was hunky-dory. He looked over at Holly. "We'd better go inside. Jarvis believes it is his duty to escort me into the house, no matter how many times I've told him we aren't living in the nineteenth or twentieth century anymore. He'll stand out in the rain waiting for us until we go inside."

He watched her head toward the manor as though she had been there before. She'd been traveling for hours and should have been dead on her feet, and yet she looked full of energy. Jarvis raced to keep up with her as he held the umbrella over her head. She'd said the bookstore had rejuvenated her, and it sure looked that way. Well, she might be full of energy, but she was forgetful. She'd forgotten her suitcase.

He got out of the auto and retrieved it from the back seat, pulling it toward the entrance. Holly stood in the center of the circular driveway and turned toward him. His heart caught in his throat. Rain was pouring down around her, her face was flushed, and her hair hung in damp ringlets around her shoulders. There were even smudges of mascara under her eyes. The impulse to drape his jacket over her shoulders, pull her into an embrace, and kiss her rushed over him in hot waves.

"You grew up here," she said over the sound of rain splashing on the cobblestones. "You must have felt like a prince. This place is amazing. Do you have servants and stuff?"

He rolled her suitcase toward her over uneven cobblestones, nodding toward Jarvis. "We don't consider Jarvis and his wife, Clara, our servants; they're part of our family. Their ancestors have worked for our family almost as long as the Atteberrys have been on this land."

"And fought beside your family when needed," Jarvis added. "Your room is ready for you, Miss Lane. Would you like to have a bite to eat before the evening meal? We have roasted suckling pig in honor of your arrival."

She hesitated a few breaths. "You've gone to a lot of trouble. Thank you so much. But I ate on the plane and I'm afraid I'm not very hungry. I'd love a tour of the manor, though."

Noel suspected Holly's sudden pale complexion was caused when she heard Jarvis announce the dinner menu. Perhaps she wasn't a big fan of suckling pig and was being polite when she said she wasn't hungry.

"Understandable," Noel said. "I'm never hungry after a long flight. Touring the manor is my father's expertise. He loves showing people around and talking about our ancestors. Like most families, we've had our share of saints and sinners."

"Begging your pardon, sir, but your father left a short time ago. He said something about following your advice, and to give you this." He paused and handed Noel a second envelope also. "You had another message from Lady Catherine Montgomery."

Noel tightened his jaw, slipping the messages into the pocket of his jacket. He'd read both later. "Thank you, Jarvis. Holly, you've had a long flight. Clara could bring something to your room if you'd like. I have business I need to address tonight, and I don't think I'll be good company. I promise we'll have a proper English dinner soon." It surprised him how much he wanted to see her again.

Chapter Ten

As Holly followed Jarvis up a winding staircase and down a long corridor with tall ceilings and mahogany paneling, her imagination went into hyper speed. Jarvis had mentioned a message from a Lady Catherine Montgomery. Holly could have written Noel's reaction in one of her novels. This woman was an ex-girlfriend. She'd written this plot before. Drop-dead gorgeous guy, new girl introduced into his life, and an ex-girlfriend who turned up out of the blue. Built-in conflict and drama. A spike of jealousy shot through her. When Holly was the author, she could control the outcome, making sure the guy and the new girl overcame their hurdles and got together in the end.

She shook away the fantasy and reminded her practical self she was here on business, not romance. Once she and Noel began working to finish their novel, there wouldn't be time for Mr. Gorgeous. Besides, this was real life. Happily-ever-afters weren't a sure thing.

Holly felt as though her legs were made of lead as she followed Jarvis down another corridor. Still, her imagination reasoned, even though this was the first time they'd met face to face, she felt as though she'd known Noel a long time, instead of a few hours. That was probably because they'd been corresponding with each other for the past year. That had to count for something.

What was more, her imagination, long in hibernation, had started to awaken, which she attributed to the English countryside and the manor. The impulse to find a cozy little corner window seat, with tea, a plate of scones and clotted cream, like her mother had suggested, and her laptop computer, flooded over her. The real test would be when she and Noel started working on the novel, but she had a good feeling that, at least on her part, the writer's block was lifting.

Jarvis paused at the end of the corridor, holding the door open as he made a slight bow for her to enter. After she stepped over the threshold, he rolled in her luggage, set it on the bench seat by her bed, and opened the drapes. "This is your room. We knew you'd want good light. It has a view of the gardens, although there isn't much in bloom this time of year."

"It's wonderful. Thank you." Holly took a quick peek around the room. High ceilings, wide moldings painted the color of cream, pale rose-print drapes with matching bedspread, and a window seat between two banks of bookshelves. A lot of pink and cream. What was missing were Christmas decorations. In fact, since entering the manor she hadn't seen any indication of the holiday season.

Did Noel object to Christmas decorations? Or was he too busy to think about such things? She refused to consider that he didn't like Christmas. "Jarvis... Does Noel... That is, how does he feel about Christmas decorations? I didn't see a tree when I came in. Is it in another part of the manor?"

Jarvis' eyes crinkled in a smile. "As a lad, Noel loved everything about the holidays and helped his mother decorate the tree. After she died, he lost interest.

That said, my Clara and I think enough time has passed and sense he misses the Christmas cheer."

"So he wouldn't object to a tree?"

Jarvis beamed. "It is my opinion that he would consider it a brilliant idea. He and his father would make a day of it. They'd go out and select a tree from the property and have it brought back to the manor to decorate."

"I love the idea. Should I bring it up, or will you?"

"Let's just see how the week progresses, shall we? The lad has a lot on his mind these days."

She nodded, noting that Jarvis seemed evasive. It was obvious that he wanted the tree, but did Noel? The last thing she wanted to do was spring the idea on Noel without knowing if a tree brought back painful memories. She knew from their emails that his mother had died of cancer when he was a child. Holly understood the pain of losing a parent so young.

Changing the subject, she indulged her imagination and said, "Will the Lady Catherine Montgomery be joining us for dinner the day after tomorrow?"

Jarvis' mouth pulled down at the corners in a frown. "Perhaps. The lad has had a tough time keeping the estate running. There never seems to be enough money, and she might be willing to offer a solution. Will that be all?"

"Yes, thank you."

He bowed again and said, "Might I say that Clara and I are very pleased you are here during the holidays. Already, this musty old manor feels as though it has received an infusion of life. There is a grandfather clock in your room, but if the chimes keep you awake, let me know and I'll take care of it for you." He then closed the door behind him, leaving Holly alone in the bedroom and the silence.

She looked at the door for a moment, going over Jarvis' parting words. He and his wife cared for Noel like family. That was crystal clear. They were also worried about him. Noel had not been what she'd expected. Interviews about him painted a picture of an aloof English bachelor. No mention was ever made about how much he cared about the people on his estate, or how hard he worked to keep his home running. She liked this side of him.

She yawned and crawled onto the bed, exhausted after the long flight, but her mind wouldn't stop spinning. There had always been the contrast between Noel's bio and the man she had gotten to know via his emails. But she'd expected that to change when she met him. It hadn't. Not in the least, which was confusing. Then learning about a mystery woman and Noel's financial woes only increased her curiosity. Somehow the woman was connected to the money situation, and Holly didn't like that one bit.

She stretched out on the bed and pulled a blanket over her as she yawned again. No, she didn't like this mystery woman one bit.

Chapter Eleven

In the wee hours of the morning, Holly roamed the downstairs halls, officially lost. Portraits of generations of Atteberrys stared down at her. The people were painted larger than life, the women wearing beautiful dresses covered in pearls and precious gems, while the men sat astride horses and held swords. The biggest takeaway was that no one smiled.

She knew from her research that there were likely at least two reasons. One, that the people had to sit for long hours and it was exhausting enough to hold a pose, let alone try to keep a smile plastered on their faces. The second was that they were embarrassed about the state of their teeth.

She shuddered as she turned down another hallway. Her goal was to find the kitchen. She was starving and had caught the aroma of baked bread and coffee brewing. Jet lag was not her friend. She'd gone to bed at a reasonable hour only to wake up at two o'clock in the morning, and since she couldn't get back to sleep, she'd tried to write.

For a solid hour she'd attempted to work on the last scenes in the novel she and Noel were writing together, but she'd hit one roadblock after another. She wanted the characters to say they loved each other, but every time she set up the scene, something happened to change the topic.

Frustrated, she gave up in favor of writing the western with Amber Rose and Douglas Greyeyes, hoping the romance would get her mind in a better space. She'd used the technique of writing a new story before when a current project was causing writer's block. And the moment she'd begun the western, the story ideas flew.

Holly had been able to picture Amber and Douglas clearly. Amber's train had arrived in the station in the predawn hours. She was ready when it rolled to a stop, her valise with her prized possession of books in her hand. She was nervous since this was the first time she'd been away from home. Her parents had died from influenza and their home had been repossessed by the bank.

Job opportunities for a woman in nineteenth century Philadelphia were paltry at best, so when Amber read the advertisement in the newspaper for a schoolteacher in Butte, Montana, she sent a telegram with her credentials. The offer of a job came the same day as a marriage proposal from the same banker who'd repossessed her parents' home. She'd turned down the proposal and spent the last of her money on a train ticket to Butte. When Amber stepped off the train, a man emerged from the mist, so unbearably tall that he took her breath away.

Holly bypassed writing scenes where Douglas introduced Amber to the town and went straight to the sex scene. Hours sped by, but when Holly's description of Douglas resembled Noel, she knew she was in trouble. When Douglas suddenly developed an English accent, Holly shut off her computer and decided it was time for a change in scenery.

And since it was almost dawn, searching for food seemed a logical solution.

Rounding a corner in the hallway, the smell of coffee grew stronger, and she heard the clatter of pots and pans. The kitchen was what she'd pictured from her obsession with watching the Downton Abbey series.

"You're up early."

She spun in the direction of Noel's voice. Had he grown taller? Were his shoulders broader? One of the sex scenes she'd started to write sprang into her thoughts, and her face heated. Douglas had taken off his shirt and was in the process of shedding his jeans to swim naked in a secluded lake. She'd made a note to do research later on when jeans were invented. Unaware of Douglas, Amber was on the other side of the lake removing her clothes.

Holly cleared her throat and ordered her vivid imagination to get a grip on itself. "Jet lag," she said trying to steady her voice. "You're up early as well."

"Habit. My mind starts racing with everything that needs to get done around here." He paused. "I made coffee."

She sat at the long table in the center of the kitchen while he poured steaming coffee into her mug. He then took a loaf of cinnamon bread out of the oven. The smell of baked bread and brewed coffee, combined with how easy it was to talk to Noel, filled her with an unexpected warmth. She'd always loved mornings with her parents, with the simple small talk and the loving glances they gave each other when they thought no one was watching.

Some romance novels highlighted fancy dinners or gifts of flowers or jewelry as examples of romance.

Holly believed it was the thoughtful moments in between those events where the real romance lived. Like a man pouring you a cup of coffee.

"Stop!"

"You don't want cinnamon bread?" Noel said.

She blinked and shook her head, then nodded. "Sorry. I was in my head, plotting a story or thinking about my characters or something like that." She took a sip of the strong coffee to wake her up and help her focus. "My ex found it annoying."

Noel narrowed his gaze. "You broke up with Derek, then?"

"I have longer relationships with my characters than with my boyfriends. Pathetic."

"You haven't found your soulmate is all," Noel said, setting a plate with a thick slice of cinnamon bread slathered with melting butter before her. "Isn't that something you'd write in your novels?"

She smiled. "You're right. That's exactly what I'd write."

"For the record, I'm glad he's the ex."

Her thoughts dwelled on his comment that he was glad she had an ex. "This bread looks delicious. You run an estate, are a bestselling thriller author, and you cook. That should be in your bio."

He sat down next to her. "I reheat, I don't cook. Clara made the bread and wrote out detailed instructions. Speaking of bios..." He paused. "Never mind. It's really none of my business."

"Mmmm?" she mumbled with a mouthful, then sipped coffee and swallowed. "This is the best I've ever tasted. My mother would love the recipe. Now, what is none of your business? Are you talking about my bio or yours? Because if it's yours, I have a few questions. For starters, are you really an international playboy with a dozen or more race cars and houses all over Europe?"

He leaned back, his bread untouched. "Don't I fit the bio?"

She wiped crumbs and butter off her fingers with a linen napkin. "You didn't pick me up from the airport in a race car, or even a high-priced luxury car. Next, you don't wear designer clothes, and you need a haircut."

He laughed softly. "You are very observant. Maybe I have race cars parked somewhere else, and who's to say I don't own houses all over Europe?"

"Do you?"

"No," he said with a roll of his eyes. "I find the whole idea of multiple homes a waste of money. For me, it fits into the same category as having more cars than you need."

"If you don't embrace that lifestyle, why hint at it in your bio?"

"My editor felt that's what readers expect. Although I love my hermit-style life, many consider it boring. A typical day for me is getting up at dawn to take care of the horses and tend the grounds. I'll write from around lunchtime until dinner, and so it goes the next day, and the day after that. What about you? Your bio is similar to mine, and I quote, 'Holly Lane follows her muse to either find love or research her novels from the wilds of Alaska to the exotic Far East.' "

She smiled. "Busted. I guess we're both fakes."

He shrugged, taking a bite of his bread. "Not fakes. We're writing hermits who are homebodies at heart and guard our privacy." He glanced out the kitchen window to the awakening sky. "As much as I'm enjoying our time here together, I need to feed the horses and repair a section of the stable's roof before the next storm."

"You do a lot on the estate on your own."

"Who better? Besides, it's expensive to hire contractors every time something breaks, and with a place this old, there is always something breaking."

"Is what Jarvis said true? Are you strapped for cash?"

Noel pushed away from the table and set his dishes in the sink. "I could rage about how inappropriate it was that Jarvis told you, but the truth is that I'm glad. I'm tired of pretending that everything is okay. Despite this big estate, we have problems like everyone else. The place is falling apart. Too many generations of neglect. Spending money on new cars, parties, or extravagant vacations helped keep up appearances better than buying a new roof or boiler. Some of my ancestors even sold off priceless art to pay for their extravagances. All that's left is a bunch of old junk and faded paintings."

Noel's reference to what remained in the manor as junk gave her an idea. Her mother was considered a genius when it came to raising money for her church and the neighborhood school district through auctions. All year long she'd accepted donations from the community, items people no longer wanted. She had a real eye for what an item was worth and what it would sell for at auction. Her mother loved the motto that said one person's junk was another's treasure.

"Would you consider selling any of what you call 'junk' if it meant the proceeds could help restore the manor?"

"In a heartbeat. What do you have in mind?"

"We'll hold an auction, but I'm going to need help. Would it be okay if I invite my mother and stepfather?"

Chapter Twelve

The air was frosty with the promise of snow as Jarvis dropped Holly off at the bookstore and café. Instead of writing at the manor, she'd decided to go into the village. Noel had said her whole family was welcome for Christmas if that's what she wanted. His generosity warmed her heart. It was as though he longed for his home to be filled with people. He said he was a hermit, but maybe there was a part of him that was lonely.

The phone call to her brother Patrick had gone as Holly expected. He was thrilled to book flights. He had been wanting their mother and stepfather to travel more, and this opportunity offered the perfect excuse. Patrick said he only wished he and his wife could visit as well, but with expecting their first child in the next couple of weeks and the doctor ordering bedrest, there was no way.

She opened the door to the café and was welcomed by the hum of conversation, the warm fragrance of basil, oregano, and rosemary simmering in the soup served to the patrons, and the glow of a cheery fire. It was between two and three in the afternoon, and the café was packed.

Mable waved hello and directed Holly over to a corner table by the window. When she reached the table, she paused. There was a reserved sign that read

"Noel Atteberry." The irrational summersault her heart made when she saw his name annoyed her. She was a grown woman, not a girl with a crush on a football quarterback. She had left the manor to clear her head—and failed.

Mable navigated around the tables and met Holly with a warm smile as she flipped over the sign. "The table is yours. Noel isn't coming today. Stay as long as you like."

Holly nodded, not sure if she was relieved or disappointed. "He must come here often if he has a table reserved."

"My café is his writing space. He said the manor is too distracting. He hears a creak when he walks across the floor or sees water dripping from the roof and feels he needs to tend to the repairs instead of writing. And there is also the issue of watching over his father. He says that in my café he feels like he can write undisturbed. Well, now, I've probably gone and said too much. It's just that, after reading all your novels, you seem more of a friend than a stranger. You're nothing like your bio, by the way."

Holly smiled. "So I've been told. What is wrong with Noel's father. Is he ill?"

"In a way. He has a compulsion to gamble. That's one of the reasons the estate is in such a sad state." The door to the café opened and a party of six entered. "Oh, my, this frigid weather is bringing in a crowd today. If you don't mind, I'll be right back to take your order."

"Take your time. I haven't had a chance to read over the menu, and I have a call to make." As Mable left, Holly picked up her phone to dial her mother and stepfather. It would be early in the morning in Seattle, but they were both early risers. Mable had given Holly another reason to get her parents to make a transatlantic flight at the spur of the moment. Yes, the idea of spending Christmas with their daughter and helping Noel dig out from under a mountain of debt would be reason enough. However, Mable had provided what Holly hoped would be the closing argument.

She knew that before her stepfather and mother met he'd been in a recovery program. Ever since, he had been an advocate for all those who struggled with different types of addiction.

The line on the other end connected, and her mother answered. "Holly, is that you?"

"Yes, Mother. Is Dad there? I have something I'd like to talk to you both about."

Chapter Thirteen

She unzipped her suitcase and pulled out her dresses, selecting the strapless black sheath. She rummaged around in her suitcase, hoping she'd packed her cute shoes—the ones with the sky-high heels, and discovered a forest-green scarf with an embroidered poinsettia. She smiled, knowing it was her mother's doing. Holly used the scarf like a tablecloth and draped it over the wood table between two wing-backed chairs. Immediately, her room took on a more holiday mood.

She laid out the black sheath, then questioned her choice. She had other dresses that weren't as revealing. But they were also boring and didn't seem to fit how she was feeling.

She set out her push-up bra and barely-there black-lace panties. Why did it matter what she wore to dinner? Her face heated until she was convinced her skin matched the color of the roses on her bedspread. She knew the answer the moment the question popped into her thoughts as she unashamedly reached for the matching black lace lingerie and headed to the bathroom to shower.

The answer was Noel Atteberry.

****

Noel poured himself a glass of red wine from a decanter on the buffet while Jarvis and Clara stood waiting as tall and still as two statues. He hoped Holly wouldn't be late.

He'd been late for dinner only once growing up. He had been twelve and had been out riding with his friends. Not only had he been an hour late, but he hadn't had a chance to change for dinner. It was a few months after his mother died, and his father had retreated into himself so dramatically that it was as if his body was there but his mind in another place. A place where Noel's mother was still alive. The truth was that Noel hadn't wanted to spend time with his father over dinner. Right after his mother died, he and his father had shared their meals in silence. Before, there had been laughter and warmth and decorations for every season. That all had stopped.

The grandfather clock began its count to six o'clock. Noel glanced toward the entrance to the dining room. Framed in the entrance was Holly. Her strapless black dress hugged her curves, and her long hair hung down in waves over her bare shoulders. As though out of a dream, she moved toward him, hips swaying, red lips parted.

Noel dropped his goblet of wine.

Jarvis and Clara rushed to his side and began cleaning up the spilled wine and broken glass. He bent to help pick up the mess, grateful for something to do. Holly was there as well, bending over, asking if she could help. He kept his face averted from hers and more importantly, from her cleavage and the way her hair brushed against her skin.

Jarvis chuckled softly, a smile tugging at the corners of his mouth. "Please don't worry about this. Clara and I have things under control. We shall have your dinner brought to the library, where it will be more…intimate."

Noel glared at Jarvis, but the man simply shrugged and smiled more broadly.

"We could find the journal," Holly said.

Noel rose slowly, keeping his back to Holly as he tried to bring his breathing under control. If the journal was half as salacious as the few lines Catherine had read to him, the last thing he wanted to do was read it aloud with Holly right now. He'd grown to like her while they worked on the book. He liked how much she cared for her family and always put them first. He'd seen her author promo picture, and it hadn't done her justice. It didn't reflect her kindness and consideration and intelligence. Seeing her tonight, dressed as she was, had been a jolt. She had a sexy side that had taken him by surprise. Did she know how attractive she was?

Reading from the journal *Whispers on a Pillow* was a terrible idea.

He swallowed. "I don't think reading the journal tonight is such a good idea, and it might not be there anymore. It would be like looking for a needle in a haystack. How about we search for it tomorrow?"

"Are you referring to the journal called *Whispers on a Pillow*?" Jarvis said. "I overheard you mention it to Miss Holly when she arrived. I've set it aside on the desk in the library."

Noel clenched his teeth. "How very thoughtful, Jarvis."

Jarvis grinned and gave a slight bow. "I aim to please, sir."

Chapter Fourteen

Holly walked beside Noel to the library in silence. His arm brushed against her bare shoulder, making normal breathing a challenge. Was he aware of his effect on her? She tore her thoughts from the heat of his body so close to hers and concentrated on the beauty of the manor.

The walls were the same dark mahogany as the hallways on the way to her bedroom. Portraits of somber-faced ancestors hung on both sides. She knew they had sat for hours with the painter, but their expressions gave the impression that there had been nothing to smile about in their lives. Noel's home, for all its beauty, could use a little Christmas joy. It needed a tree. She was thankful she'd mentioned it to Jarvis and even more thankful that Noel had once liked the holiday season. She hoped he would discover its joyous spirit again.

She gave Noel a sideways glance. He looked as somber as his ancestors. No doubt he was embarrassed over dropping his glass when she'd made her entrance. The English prided themselves on self-control. She wasn't so naïve as to think the spilled wine had nothing to do with how good she looked. His wide-eyed expression of shock had said it all. The girly side of her felt exhilarated. No one had ever reacted to her like that before.

Once, she'd gone so far as to ask Derek if he liked her new dress. He'd paused long enough to take a second look, and then had answered with the comment that she always looked nice, adding that he liked her new hairstyle. She hadn't changed her hairstyle since college, but she'd let his comment pass.

The practical side of her cautioned her not to overreact to Noel's spilling his wine. She was already attracted to the man, and this had one-night stand written all over it. She only planned to be in England until they met their deadline, which was less than one and a half weeks away. The thought of leaving gave her an unexpected twinge of displeasure she hadn't expected. She reminded herself there was an ex-girlfriend named Catherine in the picture.

He opened the door for her to what was obviously a library. Bookshelves lined the walls to her left, the glass doors on her right opened onto a patio, and straight ahead a fire crackled and rolled over a stone hearth. Beside the fireplace was a desk with a leather-bound journal she suspected was the infamous *Whispers on a Pillow*. Despite the fire, she shivered.

"You're cold," Noel said, shrugging off his jacket and sweeping it over her shoulders.

"Thank you, but I have a shawl I can use. I don't need to take your jacket."

His grin was lopsided and a little shy as he buttoned the jacket closed across her chest. "I'm doing this for me."

She pressed her lips together, smothering her smile as she nodded. He was flirting with her, and she loved it. "Is that *Whispers on a Pillow*?"

He followed her gaze. "That's the one. Are you

sure about this?"

Holly hadn't been less sure about anything in her life. She felt like she and Noel were intruding into other people's lives.

She pulled Noel's jacket close around her. "I feel a little guilty. Like we're spying. Do you know who wrote the journal?"

"The author was anonymous and wrote about a relationship between Madelyn and a man named Willingsworth." Noel reached for the journal. "What if we look on the couple as coauthors. We are having difficulty with the romance part of the story, and this couple is our inspiration."

"That is a great idea," she said, taking the journal Noel handed her and nodding. His logic made sense. "Our hero and heroine started out with such promise. There was lots of attraction, and then as soon as they were engaged in the plot to catch art smugglers, it was all business and no romance. We spent most of the time researching the art, and almost zero on why our couple belong together. We've set up places for them to make love and there is always something or someone who distracts them. I'm willing to try anything."

Noel moved over to the fire to add more wood to the flames. "What if our couple isn't meant to be together?"

She had thought about Noel's theory regarding their couple but had rejected the idea. "People think writing a romance is as easy as following a recipe. All you have to do is put two people together, add a generous cup of attraction, a dreamy location, several pinches of conflict to make it interesting, and presto, the couple falls in love."

His shirt stretched over broad shoulders as he worked over the fire. Holly took in a deep breath, imagining how he would look without clothes. Her face heated. *Concentrate.* She opened the journal and swallowed as she read the first line in the novel.

Wearing only a smile, I joined my lover under a blanket of stars.

Holly swallowed again and closed the page.

His back still turned away Noel chuckled as he added more wood to the flames. "I'm as guilty as those people you mentioned. When my editor first proposed we work together, I thought writing a romance novel would be easy."

She resisted the impulse to open the journal and find out what happened to the young lovers. "Even time-tested recipes fail," she said, clearing her throat, "when the ingredients don't blend correctly, and that's what I think is happening to the characters in our novel. They are at odds at every step of their journey. What if we can't make it work?"

"Sometimes I think our hero and heroine are too perfect. Maybe that's why I keep wanting to end the story with an explosion. I find their perfection annoying." He dusted off his hands and joined her. "Did you find anything helpful in the journal?"

Holly felt heat rise on her face. There was no way she was going to read the section with the couple swimming naked. Avoiding that section, she opened to the back pages and old letters floated onto the carpet. She picked them up. They were addressed to Madelyn and signed from Willingsworth. She read the first line of one of the letters. Willingsworth had poured out his heart to Madelyn, speaking of his love and devotion.

"Aside from the perfection issue, our characters could learn from Madelyn and Willingsworth in how they express their affection. For example, the romantic side of me loves how Willingsworth expresses his love for Madelyn in this letter."

Noel leaned in so close their legs touched. "It looks like I might learn something from Willingsworth. It sounds like you found the good stuff."

"Good stuff?" She met his penetrating gaze. Why was it so hard to breathe? She'd been in the presence of good-looking men before. Maybe not ones who looked like they could slay dragons, but still…

As Holly held the love letters, Noel reached over and turned the page of the journal. His face was close to hers as he pointed to a paragraph. "This passage looks promising," he said as he began to read. "Moonlight bathed the lovers in silver. Bodies free of clothes and restraints, entwined, pressing, thrusting, aching…"

Holly's vision blurred, transported to a forest, under a canopy of flowering trees, where naked bodies lay on a carpet of flowers. She held her breath, swept along by the vibrations of Noel's voice as he read. He was so close his warm breath caressed her skin like silk.

As though he'd heard the beating of her heart, he turned a molten gaze toward her.

There was a soft knock on the open library door. Jarvis stood holding a tray of food. "I have brought your dinner, as suggested." He hesitated. "Did I interrupt something?"

Chapter Fifteen

A few torturous hours later, Holly closed her bedroom door behind her, leaning against the cold wood. She didn't think her body would ever cool down. When Jarvis had brought dinner to the library he'd asked if he'd interrupted something.

She fanned her face with her hand as she pushed away from the door and slipped off her heels. His comment had been an understatement. Another few minutes of listening to Noel read from the journal, his rich voice vibrating against her, his breath so close to her face, and she would have ripped off his clothes.

What was happening to her?

She and Noel had eaten the dinner Jarvis brought, and she'd said it was the best she'd ever tasted. The truth was she hadn't a clue if the meal was chicken or fish. During dinner, they'd agreed that killing their characters, aside from being overly dramatic, derailed the possibility of a sequel. They proposed to each write their version of an ending chapter and then meet in the morning.

She set the journal on the dresser by the window and pulled aside the drapes, pressing her cheek against the glass. Moonlight shone down on a clearing in the garden. Was that where the lovers from the journal had rendezvoused and made love?

She knew she wanted the story she and Noel were

writing to end with their characters naked and making love. She glanced over at the journal. She'd tucked the love letters back inside before leaving the library, with the goal of reading them again.

The author of the journal was an observer of the lives and loves of couples meeting in secret. Holly had no idea how the author had acquired the letters, but she wished she knew what had happened to Madelyn and Willingsworth. Holly also wondered if the anonymous author was Madelyn. That would explain why the letters and the entries in the journal ended at the same time. The last letter ended with a promise to run away together. Maybe Holly had missed a clue embedded in Willingsworth's message to Madelyn. Had they succeeded in escaping together? Or had their plans been discovered?

Holly changed into her nightgown, scooped up the letters, and climbed into bed. Arranging the letters by date she began to read.

"My dearest Madelyn…"

****

Holly rubbed her eyes. It was three in the morning, and she couldn't sleep. Jet lag was only part of the problem. Although she'd read all the letters, she hadn't found a clue as to what might have happened to Madelyn and Willingsworth. She hoped they'd run off together. The possibility they hadn't now tugged at her heart and made her more resolved than ever to end the story she and Noel were writing with their characters happy and together.

She looked over the chapter she'd written. It wasn't her best. Something felt missing. The hero and heroine were kissing and making all the right commitment speeches. *I'll love you until the day I die. You complete me.* Yada, yada. Should she have the hero get down on one knee and propose?

Holly dropped her head into her hands. What was wrong? Maybe she was overthinking it? Maybe it was on the page and she was too close to the story to see it. That happened sometimes.

She leaned forward to re-read her latest email from her editor. The fact that her editor was getting back to her so fast during the holidays had less to do with their working relationship and more about concern over the manuscript. The message was short and to the point. "Send the last chapter of *Love Is Lost*."

Chapter Sixteen

Guilt weighed on Holly as she raced down the stairs to meet Noel for breakfast. Her editor had asked for the last chapter, and Holly had fibbed and said it was almost finished. Holly wished. It felt as though she and Noel were farther away from finishing the chapter, not closer. To distract her mind from her guilt, she'd written another scene for their novel.

But in the bright light of day the scene seemed too erotic for the type of book she and Noel were writing. She remembered thinking that it had almost written itself—an expression she used when ideas flowed and the characters seemed to talk to her, suggesting how the story should evolve.

It seemed a nutty idea that imaginary characters an author created could suggest the direction of a story. Nutty, that was, unless the writer were talking to another author. Authors never questioned the muse, they just gave it a big warm thank you.

She reached the bottom of the stairs and rounded the corner that led to the dining room. She and Noel had agreed to share their ending chapters. Her goal was to convince him that her version was the best.

She burst into the dining room. The table had been transformed from last night's formal place settings of ornate silverware and vintage china to a more casual look of earthenware pottery in shades of cream. The one similarity was the image of the Atteberry crest on the plates and cups. The mystery was that the table had been set for three.

"Has your father returned?" Holly said.

"I wish," was Noel's curt reply.

He stood by a buffet filled with eggs, fried tomato slices, bacon, fresh fruit, breads, and orange juice. If they had been in Scotland, there would have been haggis, good only if you liked your sausage made with liver, which she did not.

"Wow, you really do live like a king," Holly said, sliding next to him as she scooped scrambled eggs with salmon onto her plate, fully aware that he had sidestepped her question regarding his father's return. She noticed a tightness in Noel's voice whenever he mentioned his father.

Noel rubbed his eyes with the heel of his hand and poured black coffee into a cup. "Late night. I was up writing. We don't usually eat like this, but Jarvis insisted. He said we need our strength." His sentences shot out clean and crisp like a laundry list, though he yawned and moved from the buffet to the table.

"I couldn't sleep either," Holly said absently, joining him at the table. "I wrote too. Writing invigorates me. What did you write?"

He eyed her for a moment, then opened his computer screen. "See for yourself."

There was a change in him this morning she couldn't pinpoint. Dark circles under his eyes proved he'd been awake most of the night. She glanced over at the vacant place setting.

She took a bite of toast and scooted her chair closer to the screen, reading the scene Noel had written. Their main characters had succeeded in recovering the missing art and had turned it over to the authorities in Greece. The thieves, however, wanted revenge and had cornered the hero and heroine in an abandoned warehouse by the docks. So far so good. The action was good, the setting well-defined, and the danger real.

She scrunched her eyebrows together, took another bite of toast, and turned to the next page on the screen. The hero and heroine were locked in each other's arms and professing their love. That was new. A good sign and not that much different from her version.

But in the next paragraph the warehouse exploded in a ball of flames.

She flinched, choking on her toast. "You killed our characters in an explosion?" she said through a series of coughing fits. "We discussed this outcome. Why would you do that?"

He finished his coffee and crossed to the buffet to pour himself another cup. "It's romantic," he said over his shoulder. "Didn't you read what they said to each other before the bomb went off?"

"Oh, so you think inserting an exchange of I love you's makes it romantic? What comes after makes a difference. And as soon as our characters said those words, you blew them into small bits of bone and brain gore."

"I never described the condition of their bodies."

"It was implied," she said, "as was the copious amount of blood splattered all over the warehouse. And to be clear, our characters are dead. That is not romantic."

"What about Shakespeare's *Romeo and Juliet*? That play is considered very romantic."

"Technically, *Romeo and Juliet* is classified as a tragedy, and I dislike the story intensely. And I repeat: our characters are dead. You killed off our hero and heroine and any hope of a sequel. That is not romantic. That is as tragic as *Romeo and Juliet*."

He rejoined her at the table. "Okay, romance police. In your version, how did you end the story?" He reached over to the pages she'd handwritten.

He wasn't taking it seriously. But that wasn't the whole story. He was hyped up on caffeine and wasn't eating.

She snatched her scene from him. "You are not going to read what I wrote until you explain why the dramatic change. Last night we agreed that killing our characters would make a sequel a challenge, if not an impossibility. *Love Is Lost* is a contemporary, romantic suspense. We pitched it to our editors as a story that involves our hero and heroine as the key characters in all three books. The only way this story works now is if we turn it into a zombie apocalypse where the characters come back from the dead."

He drained his coffee again. "I need more caffeine."

"You're not going anywhere." She reached for his arm to prevent him from leaving. "Talk to me. What changed your mind?"

He eased back down in his chair. "Catherine arrived last night. A surprise visit."

"You said that as though it's the name of a category-five hurricane."

The corner of his mouth turned up. "A good description."

She pulled her hand back as her pulse raced. "Ex-girlfriend Catherine? That Catherine? I thought you said her estate was near yours? Why did she have to stay here?" Holly tried to keep her breathing under control. The sudden arrival of an ex-girlfriend added plot to a story and increased the tension and suspense. She hated that the thought had popped into her head. She didn't want tension, she wanted calm.

"Catherine's renovating her home," Noel said as he went for more coffee. "She mentioned something about being allergic to dust."

"An allergy to dust as a reason to move into the hero's house?" Holly ground out. "How cliché." Holly sliced the fried tomato on her plate and took a bite to keep occupied with something other than Catherine. The tomato tasted mushy and cold, like the direction of this conversation. Noel was distant this morning, as though last night had never happened.

Holly wanted to ask if he'd slept with her. Had he asked Catherine to marry him? Had they set a wedding date, picked out children's names…? She squeezed her eyes shut to stop the flow of crazy, jealous thoughts. Derek had talked about his ex-girlfriends all the time, and it had never bothered her. So why did Noel's ex get under her skin?

"Catherine wants me back," he blurted.

She dropped her fork, choking on her tomato and spraying it over the tablecloth. "She can't have you."

Chapter Seventeen

The sound of her fork clattering on her plate rang in her ears as bits of tomato splattered over the tablecloth. "She can't have you," had burst from her without thought. She slapped her hand against her mouth as though trying to pull the words back.

"I'm sorry. I don't know why I said that. Of course she can have you if that's what you want. You and I are just friends," she added, her words and her pulse racing. "Less than friends, actually. We're just coauthors. Strictly business. You have your life, I have mine." She was rambling, digging herself in deeper. Her voice trembled as she said, "I had no right to say what I did."

"We're not *just* friends." He reached for her hand. "And you had every right. Like you said, we're friends, and I like to think we might be more than friends. I've shared things with you that I haven't shared with anyone else, including that sometimes love is not enough."

She remembered when he'd first made that statement. He'd made it in the same email as the one in which he mentioned his breakup with Catherine when they were in college. Holly had felt the heartache in his words and had felt an instant dislike for the person who had caused him pain. She knew from previous emails that Catherine was a darling of the paparazzi. According to the tabloids, Catherine was model-perfect and had moved on from her literary boyfriend, as Noel was described, to a race-car driver, and in a matter of what seemed minutes. Holly shook away images of Catherine as she thought of what Noel had said.

He'd said that he hoped they were more than friends. So did she.

Her pulse rate, already on high alert, kicked up a dozen notches. More than friends? Did that mean he cared for her? Whoa. Slow down. Moving too fast. She felt lightheaded and sat up straighter. Could it be true? Did she also consider Noel more than a friend? She poked at another fried tomato on her plate. How much more? He was easy to look at. She could picture him on the cover of a romance novel, bare-chested, face in the shadows, a castle in the background, kissing her until her knees went weak.

When their editors first had proposed the collaboration, she'd fantasized about him and whether he looked as sexy as he sounded in his emails. She'd searched the internet for a picture of him—with no luck. The man was a recluse, which had only added to his appeal. He had managed to avoid being photographed with Catherine, which he'd said was one of the reasons she'd dumped him. In addition to dubbing Noel Catherine's literary boyfriend, the press had suggested that Noel also might be imaginary. According to Noel, that had not gone down well with Catherine.

Derek had accused Holly of spending more time with Noel than with him. She couldn't deny his comment and had told Derek he had nothing to be jealous about. After all, she'd never met Noel or seen what he looked like. That was until now. They'd worked together for almost a year, exchanging emails at least a few times every day. She searched her memory. What did she really know about him? For example, what was his favorite meal?

The answer popped into her head: Irish lamb stew with brown soda bread, along with the memory of his email where he had jokingly demanded that she vow never to tell anyone that an Englishman preferred Irish food.

Did she know his favorite color?

Green and red. Christmas colors. Her favorites as well.

His favorite vacation place was the Scandinavian countries, because he liked the cold. He wanted to name his children Jacob and Sarah...

She squished the tomato with her fork, knowing her thoughts had spiraled out of control.

"Wait. What do you mean 'love isn't enough'?"

Noel poured himself another cup of coffee and joined her. "Don't you think we should be getting to work? We have a deadline." He reached for the scene she'd written.

He was ignoring her question. Not fine. "This is a first draft," Holly said. "I need to fill in a few more details."

His head was bent as he turned the page. "There are lots of details already."

She tore a corner off her cold toast and added butter and blackberry jam. She wasn't hungry, but she needed the distraction, as well as the comfort of a sugar high. No matter how many books she wrote, that little voice inside her head always questioned if she was a good writer.

She added another spoonful of jam to her toast and took a bite. "What do you think?"

He looked up and cocked an eyebrow. "I have a few questions."

She swallowed and took a sip of tea. "Awesome. I'm open to any suggestions. I wrote this very late last night."

He nodded, stacking together the papers she'd written. "I have an orchestration question."

"Orchestration? But the characters are making love."

He cocked his head. "An editor once told me that fight scenes and sex scenes are similar. All the body parts need to be moving in the right way. She suggested a writer act out a scene whenever possible."

She looked in the direction of the kitchen to make sure Jarvis and Clara weren't about to make a surprise entrance. She lowered her voice. "I wrote a sex scene."

"Yes, you did."

"And you're suggesting we act it out?"

"Consider it research."

She snatched the papers back, flipping through the scene. "What did I do wrong?" She stared at the pages. "I know I can expand the setting, but all the body parts are where they should be. These people are having sex. I may not have had that many partners, but I have had sex, and I know what it looks and feels like. What am I missing?"

Noel put his hand over hers. "You just said it. You wrote a sex scene. But you didn't write a love scene. I know, because my editor has made it clear that my attempts at love scenes are, in her words, 'an abysmal failure.' When she first suggested I collaborate with you, I agreed only after I'd read your novels. Impressive."

A morning beam of light peeked through the lace window curtains to settle on the dining room table. She'd never guessed that he'd read any of her novels. She'd received compliments from her readers, and each one meant a lot to her. Receiving praise from a fellow author like Noel, however, spoke to the core of her writer's soul.

She blinked to clear her vision. "Thank you."

"You are very welcome. You're a talented writer. I may not be able to write romance myself, but thanks to you I know it when I read it. But these characters are only going through the motions. I half expect to turn the page and see them saying their goodbyes. I felt their frustration but not their heat. How do your characters feel about each other?"

She let out her breath. "You sound like my editor. She even went so far as to say that maybe I should stop writing romance. I think that's why we were paired together. If characters are trying to save the world, there's little opportunity for romance. A writing instructor told me to write what I know."

"Ouch."

Holly chuckled. "The longest relationship I've ever had is with you. Our one-year anniversary is January first. I keep thinking that I'll never have what my mother and stepfather have, and I'm terrified of making the wrong decision."

"You and I keep people at a distance. If this were a romance novel, Holly Lane, how would your characters overcome these obstacles?"

Holly reached for the pages Noel had stacked

together. "I'd create a series of scenes where they'd have to spend time together to solve a problem. In solving the problem, they'd discover they were in love."

Noel eased the papers from Holly's hand. "As I see it, the problem our characters face is that they don't know how to make love. And *Whispers on a Pillow* is the perfect how-to book. Think of it as research."

Was her face as red as it felt? "We are not using that journal for research. And you misinterpreted what I said. Our characters are not going to have sex as a way to get to know each other better."

He lifted an eyebrow. "What better way is there to get to know a person you are attracted to than to have sex?"

"*Omigosh*, that is such a *guy* thing to say. Are you seriously talking about our characters? Or us? Never mind. Don't answer that question. To be clear: you and I are *not* having sex, if that's what you're suggesting."

"Not sex. Love."

Holly huffed out a breath. "Okay, that sounded a lot like a pickup line. We are not making love, either."

He grinned. "It was worth a shot."

Holly glanced over the pages. "Unless… How do you feel about foreplay?"

"Is that a trick question?"

The door to the dining room opened, and a woman stood in the entry—white-blonde hair, high cheek bones, perfect makeup. Wearing a gold-toned wool sheath with white piping under a matching ankle-length coat, she glided into the room. Holly could imagine a casting director choosing this woman for the lead role of another remake of a movie about Princess Diana.

Holly knew who she was by the authoritative strut in her walk as she entered the room and the possessive way she glanced toward Noel. No introductions needed. This was Catherine, Noel's ex-girlfriend from college. He'd only mentioned her once, but the description had stuck in Holly's head.

"Am I interrupting?" Catherine asked in a practiced tone. Clearly, she'd said these words before, knowing full well she was interrupting but not caring.

Holly decided to dislike her.

Noel's expression looked frozen as he stood and gave Catherine a slight nod. "Lady Catherine, I would like to introduce you to the coauthor I told you about, Holly Lane."

Chapter Eighteen

Lady Catherine stepped forward on impossibly high heels as Holly pulled her tunic-style cable-knit sweater over her yoga pants. She'd curled her hair, added modest makeup, and finished off the look with long dangling hoop earrings. After numerous outfit changes this morning, she'd settled on this one, which she hoped telegraphed the right combination of serious writer and womanly charms.

She'd thought about wearing a cute dress or skinny jeans and a silk blouse, but she worried Noel might get the wrong impression and think she was trying to get his attention romantically—which of course she was. They weren't on a date, she rationalized, they were meeting to work on their novel. If he had told her his ex-girlfriend would be meeting them later, would that have made a difference in what she wore?

Absolutely.

Holly resisted the temptation to take notes. This wasn't a character in one of her novels; this was a flesh-and-blood person, and her competition.

Competition?

The word stuck in her thoughts as though it had been super-glued. Why had she used that word? Was she falling for Noel? The answer to that question was swift. Of course she was. Holly took mental notes on Lady Catherine so she could write the woman into a novel as an example of the perfect villainess.

Except Catherine didn't look like a villainess. She looked nice, despite all her perfectness. Was that a word? And hadn't Noel said that his ex-girlfriend used her time and resources to help single moms? Drat. Now, Holly couldn't dislike her.

Lady Catherine approached the table and held out her hand in greeting. "It is very nice to meet you." Her voice was as perfect as her appearance.

"It's nice to meet you, as well," Holly said, hoping the tone of her voice sent the message to Catherine that Noel was off limits.

The smile Catherine offered was a challenge. Message received. Message returned.

"Are you staying for breakfast?" Noel said.

"You know the only thing I have for breakfast is tea, but I don't even have the time for that. I can't stay. I have a meeting in town with my solicitor." She stood on tiptoe and gave Noel a peck on the check. Turning on her heels, she left as quietly as she'd appeared.

Instead of feeling as though things were back to normal, Holly had the impulse to repeat a Star Wars phrase: "There is a disturbance in the force."

A few seconds ticked by before Holly found her voice. "She seems nice." The comment was lame, but she couldn't say what was really on her mind. She wanted to ask Noel why Catherine was back in his life.

He poured himself another cup of coffee. "The real reason for Catherine's visit was to ask if I'd reconsidered. It was late when we finished talking, and I suggested she stay the night."

Holly bypassed the first question she wanted to ask Noel, which was if Catherine had spent the night in his room. Readers complimented Holly on her vivid imagination and plot twists. Right now her imagination was a curse, not a blessing.

She decided to take the high road and avoid the question of where Catherine had slept. "Can I ask what she wanted you to reconsider, or am I out of line?"

"You might as well know. My father borrowed a lot of money from Catherine's husband to maintain his expensive habits. He put up as collateral the entire contents of the estate, which included paintings and furniture. Her husband's will stipulated the loan must be repaid by the arranged date, one year from his death, or the whole estate will be turned over to Catherine."

Holly paused, taking in Noel's dark mood. "Now I know why your reaction was to blow our characters into a thousand tiny pieces."

****

The breakfast buffet was cleared away, leaving only the tea and coffee service, as she and Noel sat in a strained silence. Holly had asked if Jarvis had any shortbread, wishing she had included chocolate in the request. She hadn't mentioned Catherine's visit again, knowing that Noel would bring it up when he was ready.

Jarvis returned and set before her a heaping plate of shortbread cookies with wafer-thin squares of dark chocolate at one side. "Mr. Noel said you couldn't write without your chocolate."

"So true." Holly snatched a square from the plate and mouthed her thank you to Jarvis and Noel. The smooth texture melting in her mouth gave her the infusion of sugar she needed in her bloodstream. "Do you want to work on our scene again?"

"I'm not sure." Noel combed his hands through his hair. "I have a hard time concentrating right now. My father is trying to get help for his problem. That's what the note Jarvis gave me was all about. My father said that he would be staying in town while he seeks counseling. I want to believe him. I want it to be back the way it was. In the note, he also suggested I marry Catherine. My father has always been about the easy way out and the quick fix." Noel broke a shortbread cookie into two pieces, placing both halves on his plate uneaten, looking as though the responsibilities he carried might crush him.

She understood a little about the cost of mounting bills. Her parents' medical expenses had almost resulted in the loss of their home. They were lucky they had family and resources. True, she had paid off the mortgage, but her brothers were there as well. They had all pulled together. Noel was alone.

As much as it bothered her, she said, "Is that what you want to do? Marry Catherine?"

He met her gaze. "A short time ago, you told me I couldn't. Are you giving me your permission?" There was an edge of sadness in his voice and something else.

She sighed. Her comment that she didn't want him to marry seemed a lifetime ago and was before she knew why he might consider Catherine's offer. If they married, their lands would be joined, and the conditions of the will met. He and Catherine had a history together. Did Noel still have feelings for Catherine? "You didn't answer my question. Do you want to marry Catherine?"

He leaned toward her. "No, I do not want to marry Catherine."

The relief she had expected was short lived. Regardless of how Noel felt, he was backed into a corner with two options: marry Catherine or lose his home.

Holly reached for the shortbread Noel had broken in half, added one of the squares of chocolate, and took a bite. She expected another sugar high. This time it tasted like cardboard. "How much money do you need to pay off the loan?"

He broke the remaining shortbread half into crumbs. "A small fortune, and before you offer to help us, you already told me you depleted your savings by paying off your parents' mortgage. I've sunk all my money into this place, as well, and have been working day and night to reestablish horse breeding here as a way to pay off the bank loans my father made. At one time this estate was famous for horse breeding, and given time, I believe it will be again. Before I learned about the will, I thought there might be a chance to save the estate. Now I'm not at all sure."

"That was the reason you were always late sending me pages to review. I was a terrible nag, always bugging you to send me a new scene or review one I had written."

He shook his head. "You were not a nag. In fact, your emails were the bright spot of my day. You were kind when I was late and said encouraging things to me, like 'inspiration is not a switch that can be turned on or off, it needs to be nurtured and respected,' or 'the muse is shopping for ideas, and when she returns your words will flow.' "

She remembered those emails. Her phrases were as much for herself as they were for Noel. She finished her cookie, wiped her hands on a napkin, and reached to hold his hand, at a loss for words. What would Noel do? Marrying for money seemed medieval: a plotline she might write in a historical novel. And in the novel the two people would fall in love. She groaned. What a mess.

Jarvis emerged from the kitchen with a fresh pot of coffee and cleared his throat. "Pardon my interruption, sir, but I couldn't help overhearing your conversation with Miss Lane. There is the matter of your mother's little hobby."

"Yes, Jarvis, I'm aware. You've mentioned it before, and I'm thankful for your concern. I know you're trying to help." He turned toward Holly. "You would have liked my mother. She was more interested with the history connected to the items she collected than their monetary value."

"Yes, indeed," Jarvis said. "She collected everything from first edition Hemingway novels to vintage clothes by Coco Chanel. She particularly liked Picasso's history and that his father made his son learn to paint in the style of the old masters before experimenting in his own style. I believe she purchased one of his paintings."

Chapter Nineteen

"Picasso?" Holly said, nearly jumping to her feet. "What are we waiting for?"

For a dose of reality, Noel wanted to add. Jarvis' comment regarding his mother's collection of art sounded like the perfect solution—sell a priceless portrait and save the estate. Added bonus: Noel wouldn't have to marry Catherine. But things were never that simple.

Holly was on her feet and holding her hand out toward him. "We should find your mother's art and have an appraisal done."

He pushed away from the table and stood. "That won't be necessary. As I've told Jarvis over and over, anything worth selling my father sold long ago, but it wasn't enough. He still had to borrow money from Catherine's husband."

"So we're back where we started."

Noel liked that Holly considered this her problem as much as his. He'd been serious when he told her he considered her more than a friend. He hadn't meant to say it aloud. He knew from her emails that she was as skittish as he was when it came to commitments. Maybe that was why they had connected so easily. Their work came first, and a relationship challenged their writing time.

Over the time they'd been writing together, they'd

discussed people they were dating and admitted their relationships were always superficial. Holly confessed in one email that the person she was dating currently wasn't interested in discussing anything deeper than, "Where would you like to go for dinner tonight?"

Noel admitted to Holly he had experienced the same issue. What he didn't say was that he felt he didn't have the time or interest in deep conversation with a woman. It might lead to the person believing there was a chance at a commitment, and he didn't want to give her false hopes. He already had more responsibilities than he could handle right now.

Of late, he'd realized his philosophy was flawed. It could lead to a life of loneliness.

"Do you want to go for a walk?" His question surprised him as much as it must have Holly, if the startled expression on her face was any indication.

To his shock, she nodded and straightened the pages of her chapter. He stayed her hand, winding her arm through his. "Jarvis knows not to touch our work, don't you, Jarvis?"

"Begging your pardon, sir. It's about your mother's art collection?"

Noel clapped Jarvis on the shoulder. "Don't worry, old friend. There was nothing you could have done. I'm well aware that my father sold it right after my mother died."

"But, sir…"

Noel ignored Jarvis as he walked beside Holly to the entrance. Jarvis was close on his heels, grabbing coats, hats, and scarves from the hall closet. Noel opened the door to bright sunshine and the soft fall of snow. He liked the strange juxtaposition of snow falling on a sunny day. It might be his last time to walk the grounds of the estate.

Chapter Twenty

Holly leaned against the fence by the stables and soaked in a ray of sunlight that peeked through the clouds. After a tour of the grounds, Noel had headed here, asking her to wait while he double-checked the roof. She understood why Noel loved his home as much as he did. There was a timelessness about the grounds and the buildings that invited you into their world. This place could exist in either the twenty-first century or the sixteenth, and he imagined the feel would be the same as people loved and worked and lived out their lives in any era.

She had heard the pride in his voice as he showed her around the gardens and pointed out the area where he intended to expand and plant vegetables and fruit trees. Over one hundred years ago, he'd said, the estate had been completely self-sustainable, growing food and livestock: a fortress that could endure a siege. Over time, his ancestors had taken the easier path and bought what they needed from stores and local markets. Noel's goal was to restore the estate to its former glory. What was left unsaid was whether he would have the resources to achieve that goal. Their relaxed meanderings had led toward the stables, and here Noel's voice took on a new tone, one filled with love.

She tilted her face to the sun and closed her eyes. What would it be like to live here? Would she miss her family and her life in the States? She'd heard that when people traveled, they sometimes felt an immediate reaction to the place they visited. At times the impression of a place they visited spanned the emotional spectrum from comfort and ease as though moving in and settling down was the natural order, to the more negative where the person wanted to leave at once. Where were her emotions when it came to this place?

She took in another mental drink of the rare winter sunshine and glanced toward the stables. Noel walked out from the double doors. He raised his arms to gesture it was safe and to join him.

Holly had the sudden impulse to run to him, like in the previews of a romance movie where two people held out their arms and raced toward each other in a field of wildflowers. For some reason there was always a field and a passionate kiss. Except she wouldn't be running over a dry field, she'd be sloshing through mud puddles.

She laughed softly. That was the thing that stopped her from making a fool out of herself? Mud puddles? Worst fear confirmed. She was losing her mind. Before she'd arrived here, she'd bemoaned the possibility that she'd lost her ability to conjure romantic situations for her characters. Since arriving in England, her imagination was pouring out of her as though a dam had broken.

She picked her way around the mud puddles and vowed that the next time she visited the village she'd buy a pair of boots.

"You were laughing," Noel said. "Most people weep when they see all the mud."

She gazed up into his clear and open expression. "Plotting a scene." It wasn't exactly a white lie. There was a plot. There were characters. There was even a setting. The only problem was that the characters were her and Noel. Before he could ask penetrating questions, she said, "Your estate is beautiful." Even though she'd used the comment as a distraction, she meant it.

He took her hand and the spark of his touch shot through her. His eyes widened a little as though he'd felt something as well.

"You are one of those rare people who sees the beauty." The corner of his mouth turned up at the edges. "I love this time of year. Not everyone feels the same. Trees are bare of their leaves and fruit, gardens lie dormant, the earth turned over and drenched with rain, and everywhere you look there is mud. But there is a promise in the air that speaks of a new beginning, an end to the old ways and the start of the new."

She squeezed his hand and stepped in a mud puddle so that she could stand closer to him. "That was poetic. I love the visual you paint with your words."

He nodded slowly. "I can't claim the words as my own. My mother said that to me one winter when I was complaining about the rain. Come. I want to introduce you to the horses and our newest colt, Deadline."

"You named a colt Deadline?"

His eyebrows drew together. "Not one of my best, I'll grant you, but it fitted my mood at the time. I felt like I was drowning in deadlines."

"And you took it out on a cute little horse?" Holly walked beside him into the warm stables, rich with the smells of hay, new timber for the roof, and horses.

"Picking out a name is a serious responsibility. You can't honestly tell me you're happy with your choice, can you? We need to think of another one."

He stared at her with an odd expression. "How do you know me so well? You're right. Choosing the right name is important. Jarvis thought I was quite mad to worry about a name for a horse."

She was bathed in his gaze and never wished to leave. "Names are important. They connect us with those around us in ways that are not easy to understand. Why don't you tell me a little bit about the colt?"

"He's always running off and getting lost but is also friendly and in a perpetually good mood." Noel leaned toward her and brushed his fingers down the side of her face, touching her hair. He pulled back, his voice deep as an endless night. "There was a piece of straw in your hair."

"Your colt sounds a lot like Santa's reindeer Rudolf."

His hand still holding hers, he moved in the direction of a horse stall a short distance away. "I like the name, and maybe Rudy for short."

Holly was almost positive there hadn't been straw in her hair. He'd wanted to touch her, and she hadn't moved away because she had wanted to be touched. She walked beside him and ordered her imagination to cease and desist as it pictured Noel holding her in his arms.

Chapter Twenty-One

The afternoon sun shone through the library window and added its golden glow to the mahogany paneled room. Noel stretched his neck to the side to relax his muscles. He and Holly had been writing since breakfast. He'd first resisted, claiming that writing alongside each other wouldn't work as he wrote alone and in perfect silence. She'd said it would be difficult for her as she wrote best when in a crowded, noisy coffee shop. Then she'd hit him with some new age mumbo-jumbo about maybe the reason they weren't in sync on how to end their novel was because their writing muses weren't in the same room.

He pushed back and said there was no such thing and thought he'd made a few good points, and yet somehow here he sat at a table near the window, with Holly curled up on the sofa in front of the fireplace, researching and taking notes and looking adorable in an oversized green knit jumper over a pair of fitted jeans.

She closed the large, leather-bound book she'd been reading and rubbed her neck. As though sensing him, she slid her gaze toward him, and her eyes sparkled, crinkling at the edges. He loved that smile. It was open, no pretense.

She shifted a journal and a pad of paper off her lap. "Ready for a break?" She set a stack of books on the floor, making a space for him on the sofa.

He added another log to the fire before joining her. The move was a personal test of his self-control, as was his decision to sit as far away from her in the library as possible. He'd said it was because he needed a quiet place to write. The truth was it bothered him that being near her felt right, comfortable, peaceful. Time stopped when he was near her, and the world with all its hyper-craziness drifted away, like a fog over a lake when a breath of fresh air arrived, leaving only a mirror-smooth surface.

"Did you find out anything more about our couple in the journal?" he asked, dusting off his hands.

Her smile widened as she tucked her legs up on the sofa. "Madelyn and Willingsworth loved the Christmas season and had a lively debate over when the Christmas tree was first introduced to Britain from Germany. Willingsworth insisted it was Queen Victoria's husband, Prince Albert, who was responsible for it, but Madelyn claimed that Queen Charlotte, the German wife of George III, had Christmas trees displayed in the Royal Court as early as eighteen hundred. It seems Martin Luther started it all in the early fifteen hundreds when he noticed stars winking in and out of a forest near his home. Inspired by the sight, he cut down a tree, brought it home for his children, and decorated the tree with candles to simulate stars."

"We are not decorating our Christmas tree with candles."

"Of course not. We'd likely burn down the manor. We'll use Christmas lights."

"They are called fairy lights here in the UK."

She laughed softly. "I like that they are called fairy lights. Oh, that gives me an idea for another story."

He eased the journal out of her hand. "Madelyn's journal and the love letters are giving you too many story ideas. One book at a time, please," he said, laughing.

She tugged it back into her arms. "It's not just story ideas. We should recreate a Victorian-style Christmas in honor of our lovers from *Whispers on a Pillow*. Madelyn said they went all out, decorating every nook and cranny of the manor. I'm sure everything we need in the way of decorations and ornaments are still here." Holly sat up straighter. "And because the story we're writing takes place over Christmas, we should have a book signing while I'm here, to advertise our release next year. I'll contact Mable in town, then see what we can do about the decorations."

There was something about her enthusiasm that was contagious. But they had to be practical. She had a good idea, but what she proposed was a lot of work, and they had a novel to finish. "Holly, slow down. Let's think this through. We still haven't arrived at a consensus as to how to finish our novel."

"Consensus? Well, no wonder we're having agreement issues if you are using words like consensus to determine the fate of our characters. They are flesh and blood."

"We made up our characters in our imagination. They are not real people."

Her eyes widened, then narrowed as though her blood pressure was on a slow simmer, ready to boil. "I'll agree that our stories evolve from our imagination, but when we develop our characters, they become real to us, or they should. We have to believe our characters are flesh and blood, with feelings as complicated as

Madelyn and Willingsworth have—or you and I, for that matter. How else can we tell a story that will reach the hearts and minds of our readers?" She paused as though to catch her breath. "Did you do the exercises I suggested?"

"They didn't help," he said in a flat tone.

Her eyes lit up as though on fire as she scooted closer to him on the sofa. "Yes, they did. I can tell by your closed expression. It's like one of those heavy castle gates slammed down tight over your emotions. What did he say?"

Noel's jaw tightened. "You mean my character?"

"Yes, of course I mean Steven. You told me he's the one giving you the most trouble."

He folded his arms over his chest. "Fine. You told me…"

"Suggested," she corrected.

He inclined his head forward. "Okay, suggested that if a character was hard to develop, the interview technique might help unblock the character's motivation. The idea is to create a scene between the character and the author, posing as a therapist or reporter, and conduct a counseling session or interview."

"And?"

"And Steven told me I was full of crap."

Holly laughed softly as she pulled Noel's arms down. "You should listen to him."

"This is ridiculous." Noel pushed to his feet. "I'm the author. I'm the one in control, not Steven."

The library grew heavy with the silence. The words he'd said repeated in his thoughts as well as how he'd felt when he interviewed Steven. Noel could feel himself trying to direct his character's answers while at the same time feeling Steven resist. There was a push-pull going on. A deep-seated debate between whether people could find a happily-ever-after. Noel believed people were fools to try, while Steven disagreed vehemently.

Chapter Twenty-Two

Holly settled in the window seat of the library with Madelyn's journal as the grandfather clock began its countdown to midnight. Her jetlag had turned her days and nights upside down and sideways, and she knew sleeping was impossible. She'd tried writing, but when the scene introduced new characters like Jack the Ripper and his sidekicks, Sherlock Holmes and Watson, and a new plotline that involved finding Excalibur, Holly knew she was overtired and should give up until the morning. The perfect distraction was to find out more about Madelyn and her Willingsworth.

Each stroke of the clock's chime reverberated through Holly as she opened to the first time Madelyn and Willingsworth met. Holly had scanned the entry: now she intended to read it in more detail. According to the entry, Madelyn was in this very drawing room, painting a scene of a coach, drawn by six cloud-white horses, traveling through the snow. It was easy to visualize Madelyn.

Madelyn had tied a smock over her pale blue Victorian day dress to protect it from paint smudges and wore her hair piled high on her head. She concentrated on the canvas she'd placed on the easel as she expertly brought her painting to life. She added long shadows of sword-gray shades and low-hanging branches that clawed at the sides of the coach as it sped past, seeking escape from an unknown pursuer.

"Begging your pardon, Lady Madelyn, where would ye like me to put the crate of ornaments you ordered from the Derby factory?"

Madelyn looked up into eyes as green as the Highlands in spring. The man wore the clothes of the working class. His shirt was plain with no collar, where today's men's fashions insisted on a high starched collar that kept the chin high. Yet his bearing was remarkable. Broad shoulders and a steady expression that held one's gaze. It was hard not to stare at him. He looked strangely familiar.

"Have we met, sir?"

"Of a sort. Ye visited my place of work to order handblown ornaments. I was one of the glass blowers in the factory."

The image of a man's bare chest glistening with sweat from the forge warmed her cheeks. Madelyn had stormed into the factory unannounced when the woman in the front office had said the owner was unavailable. She'd caused a stir with her impulsive act. Men rushed to put on shirts and bow their apologies for their state of undress. Yet she was the one who had surprised them. She remembered the man standing before her as he had also reached for his shirt. But the expression on his face had been different from the others. She'd remembered that expression. It had made her feel she was the most beautiful woman he'd ever seen.

He wore it now. She remembered he'd boldly told her his name was Willingsworth.

"I do remember you." She glanced over toward the crate of round orbs. Each one was tucked lovingly into a separate compartment in the open crate. She estimated there were two dozen or more. She peeled back the tissue wrapping and discovered cream-white glass. She sucked in her breath. "But the owner said he only made apple-red ornaments, or silver, and refused my request. I was told the ornaments I wanted could not be produced."

He set the crate down at her feet like an offering to a queen and stepped back. He glanced over her shoulder at her painting. "There is emotion in every brush stroke. You have a gift."

She turned to gaze at the painting with him. The shared moment felt intimate, and her face warmed once again. "My father would disagree. He believes a woman should paint only happy scenes. He complains my little pastime costs him dear and results in more paint on my clothes than the canvas. I remind him that my allowance from my mother's estate pays to replace my wardrobe and purchase supplies, but he insists it is money ill spent."

She rubbed a smear of indigo-blue paint from the back of her hand. What had come over her? She was discussing personal matters with a perfect stranger. She cupped her hands together as though to prevent additional secrets from escaping.

"I apologize," she said. "I am keeping you from your work."

He glanced once more toward the painting. "If I may be so bold, the time with you is worth any I might lose at the glass-blowing furnace. But do not worry on my account. I will make up the lost time this evening. I am paid by the piece, and each one I make brings me closer to earning my passage to the Americas."

"You are leaving?" The thought bothered her more

than it should.

"I have seen my future in my father's bent shoulders and vacant stare," Willingsworth said. "I intend to forge a new path."

Willingsworth was ambitious. Her father would not believe a working man capable of such lofty goals. "That is commendable," she said, seeing him in a new light.

"May I also ask why it is that you wanted white ornaments?"

"My father wishes me to paint them with images of Christmas trees decorated with fairy lights and a picture of a family gathered around a warm fire."

"Fine subjects for the season. Please consider painting an image of the coach you have drawn as well." He paused. "It has spirit."

"Which is precisely why my father would not approve. He remarks that the subject is too dark for the celebration of Christmas." Her hands clasped tighter.

She gasped at her bold statement as she searched for a safer topic. She'd spoken out against her father and had painted him in a poor light. She was taught that a daughter must be obedient and voice only gratitude and love. Her father warned that servants gossiped and enjoyed spreading venom about those above their station in life. Yet Willingsworth didn't seem the sort who trafficked in gossip or other's failings.

"There must be dark before there is light," he said, interrupting her thoughts. And with a slight bow, he replaced the cap on his head. "If you have need of additional ornaments, please send word to me directly."

He bowed once more and left the drawing room, and with his leaving, the room seemed to chill and the light dim.

The grandfather clock began its countdown to a new hour as the brass pendulum ticked away the seconds. The first chime rang out.

The second chime sounded, and then the third.

Then the chimes ceased, with only the steady back and forth movement of the pendulum to break the silence.

Holly closed Madelyn's journal and stretched. It was three o'clock in the morning. The journal read like a love story. And as a hopeless romantic, Holly longed to find out what had happened to Madelyn and Willingsworth. Something held her back. As long as she didn't research too deeply into their story, Holly could imagine that the lovers lived happily ever after.

But the obstacles they faced were insurmountable, and the Victorian era had guidelines to keep people in their place. Willingsworth was from the working class and Madelyn from the upper class. Holly wanted to believe that Madelyn and Willingsworth overcame those challenges, but it didn't look good for them.

Her decision made, she replaced *Whispers on a Pillow* on the bookshelf between a volume of poetry by Elizabeth Barrett Browning and a collection of poems called *Let's See*, by Irene Redmond Zollinger. *Whispers on a Pillow* would be there, waiting for Holly, if she ever changed her mind.

Chapter Twenty-Three

The next day the grounds of the manor were soggy and wet and draped in blurred shades of moss-green and amber-gold as Holly followed the sound of chopping wood. She loved the home she'd grown up in, but this was a close second. She had ventured outside to find Noel.

The gossamer threads of the entries she'd read in *Whispers on a Pillow* were still there, teasing her to find out what happened. She'd read how Madelyn and Willingsworth first met, the conflict they'd faced, and that they'd become lovers. All that was left was to find out if they defied Madelyn's father and made a life together.

She shook her head, trying to shake the thoughts from her mind. She was doing it again. She was letting a story distract her from the current project with Noel. Every corner of the estate inspired her and spoke to her of love and romance. This morning, while gazing out of her window at the mist-covered fields, she imagined a soldier returning from war to the welcoming arms of the woman he loved.

Noel had said that he wrote after chores, but except for their one session at breakfast, she'd never seen him write a word. Perhaps he was one of those writers who waited until everyone was in bed and fast asleep.

He was at the side of the stable splitting wood. His

broad shoulders and muscular back and arms strained against the thin fabric of the long-sleeved cotton shirt he wore. In her novels she would have had the hero bare-chested. She chuckled as she approached Noel, remembering that she'd put that type of scene in a novel set in Anchorage, Alaska. Her editor had brought up the point that no matter how manly her hero, it would be insane for him to chop wood shirtless in a below-freezing blizzard. Holly had agreed, thanked her editor for her touch of reality, and rewritten the scene.

Noel leaned his axe against the chopping block and wiped sweat from his brow. "Did you get a lot of writing done this morning?"

"I did," she said, sitting down on a fallen tree trunk. "How about you? Any progress with that last chapter?"

He picked up another log to split and set it on the chopping block. "Not yet." His focus rested on the wood as he drew in a deep breath. "I'm stuck."

"If you're talking about writer's block, I can relate. Before I arrived here, I couldn't come up with one new plot idea for a novel. Now, I can't turn off the flow of ideas. You just need to give it time."

He rested the handle of his axe on his shoulder. "That's just it. What if I don't want to give it time? The estate consumes all my waking hours. I've had a good run and achieved more success than most writers. I wouldn't be the first author to call it quits, and I've felt this way for a long time. I only agreed on writing this novel with you because the advance was so generous Now, even that's in jeopardy. I've run out of ideas for novels, and that's not a good place for an author." He paused. "You deserved to know. After we turn in this novel, I'll let both my agent and my editor know that it's my last book."

He swung the axe over his shoulder and brought it down with a crack, splitting the wood in half.

She flinched at the sound and searched for a way to change his mind. He split the wood sections smaller, then reached for another wedge. She understood how he felt. Writing was a solitary occupation and could be lonely at times. Some authors got their plot ideas by working out scenarios with other authors. In other cases, plot ideas were inspired by events, people, or things. But when an author was mired in personal or family troubles, the situation could block their flow of imagination.

He'd finished chopping and was stacking the split wood on a pile. She knew the droop in his shoulders had little to do with the effort to chop wood and more with his confession to give up writing. She'd read the passion in his words, and knew to the depths of her soul that it would be harder than he realized to stop writing his beautiful stories. She couldn't let that happen. She also knew that anything she said would result in him digging in deeper. What he'd said about why he should give up writing was logical. But unless you were a writer, there was nothing logical about the whole process of how a story built in your imagination and the need to then write it down.

"I won't try to talk you out of it," she said as an idea formed.

He nodded, keeping his back turned toward her.

"You need a break and your home needs a tree. I propose we spend the day searching for the best Christmas tree we can find."

"There is a lot left for me to do around the estate."

She could hear the hesitation in his voice. Despite what he said, she sensed he was considering her offer. She seized on the opening. "Let me help with the chores that can't wait, and leave the rest for tomorrow."

He glanced toward the manor. "It would be nice to have a Christmas tree…"

She jumped off the tree stump. "Then we have a deal." She said it as a statement, not a question.

He grinned. "You won't give up until I agree, will you?"

She grinned as well, holding back the impulse of a full-on smile. She would keep her promise to ban writing from their conversation while they searched for a tree. She would, however, find another way to prove to him that he was not ready to give up writing novels.

Holly widened her grin. "I promise. I will never give up."

Chapter Twenty-Four

It felt as though she and Noel had walked for miles, with each step taking them farther away from the manor, with all the problems it represented, and deeper into a pristine, untouched area of the estate's lands. Along the way, Noel had pointed out deer eating at feeders he and his men had provided to help them survive the long winter months. He also told her the brush and grasses were kept long and thick in order to provide shelter for the foraging animals and birds.

She heard the love in each word he spoke about the lands that had been in his family for centuries. He'd talked about how much the land had meant to his father, but it was obvious that Noel was its real protector.

A half hour ago they'd entered the clearing in search of the perfect Christmas tree. A thin layer of snow frosted the ground and sparkled in the beams of the afternoon sun in incandescent forest green and berry red. Holly perched on a fallen tree trunk, rubbing behind the ears of one of Noel's Irish wolfhounds who'd tagged along. Noel shed his jacket and used his axe to point to a twelve-foot pine tree they'd selected.

"Are you sure this is the one you want?" He looked magnificent against the backdrop of the forest. A huntsman patrolling his lands, or in days gone by, he was the landowner protecting his estate from bands of marauding invaders. But strength alone wouldn't defeat what Holly suspected Noel faced. They'd avoided the topic that this might be his last Christmas on the Atteberry estate. She was adept at writing her characters out of difficult plot problems. But this was real life, and she wasn't convinced there was an easy solution for what Noel faced, and that uncertainty dampened her mood. She had to find the way out of this, if not for herself, then for Noel. If only her mother were here. Her mother was a genius when it came to raising money for worthy causes.

She understood Noel's reluctance to feel optimistic they'd find a solution that could wipe out the debts. Those types of miracles were few and far between. Holly brought her knees against her chest, committed to keeping the mood light. She was careening into Miss Debby Downer territory, and she didn't like how that made her feel. Whenever she felt like this, she wrote herself out of the funk, either by journaling or writing a scene to a new book. Maybe it would work if she brainstormed an idea with Noel: something whimsical and fun. And the most fun thing she could think of was a scene where the love interest had a romantic moment.

She cleared her throat to get Noel's attention. "I can't be positive if that is the right tree," she said with mock-seriousness. "If I were writing this scene, I'd have my hero remove his shirt."

He cocked an eyebrow. "Let me get this straight. You will know if this is the right tree if I remove my shirt?"

She batted her eyes in mock surprise. "Of course. Everyone knows that the best way to judge a Christmas tree is to ask a man without a shirt to stand next to the tree."

"I've read your novels, and no, you wouldn't ask your hero to remove his shirt unless there was a compelling reason."

She shrugged, keeping her expression stoic. "Maybe I'm venturing into new territory. Humor me."

His eyebrows drew together as his lips quirked up in a smile. "You're going to have to give me a more compelling reason to shed my clothes. It's freezing."

"Heroes never feel the cold," she said with a straight face.

His laughter burst out, then softened to a smile that reached his eyes. "What does removing my shirt have to do with selecting the right tree?"

It had zero to do with it, but he was smiling again, and that was worth the nonsensical banter. "Are you serious? As I said, everyone knows that in a romance novel the only way decisions are made, or in this case when a tree is cut down, is after the hero takes off his shirt. We might consider this for a scene in our story. Strictly for research purposes and inspiration, of course. I'm assuming you have broad shoulders and rippling abs. That is a key component for a hero."

Noel snorted. "We have had this conversation in emails, and you disagreed with heroes and heroines always being so perfect. But for the sake of this plotline, does the heroine in this story plan to sit idly by, doing nothing but watch the hero flex his muscles and chop down a tree?"

She pressed her hand against her chest as though offended. "Our heroine has plenty to do. While you, I mean, our hero, flexes his muscles, our heroine will say things, like, 'Oh, my, what big biceps you have.' "

His laughter turned mischievous as he unbuttoned

his shirt. "Having a beautiful woman watching our hero will be a turn-on. Things could get frisky."

He'd called her beautiful. His comment lingered, grew, expanded, glowed bright. What was happening? "Frisky?" she said, attempting to keep the fantasy scene alive and just pretend. "I can't believe you used that word." She also couldn't believe he was really going to remove his shirt. She had begun this exchange to lighten the mood. The expression in his eyes told her the mood might be light, but there was also building heat.

"Using the word 'frisky' is me trying to keep our scene rated P.G." He unfastened his belt and pulled it through the beltloops with a snap. "On second thought, heroes do their best work bare-ass naked."

Her face flamed. "We are not writing an erotic novel."

"We could." Noel's shirt was unbuttoned, his chest laid bare, as he moved toward her slowly.

Her breath came out in puffs of frosted air. She'd fantasized about writing a scene where the hero and heroine were lost in the passion of their growing attraction and desire for one another. Time would slip away, and consequences would be forgotten. Their kisses would become more urgent as clothes were shed and naked flesh was pressed against heated skin.

Noel reached her and stood so close his breath warmed the air as he shrugged his shirt off his shoulders. "I'm not marrying Catherine."

His statement broke the fantasy world she'd created and made it real. "Really?"

"Really."

She pulled his shirt back over his shoulders, her

fingers tingling as they grazed bare flesh. She cleared her throat. "Keep your shirt on, mister," she said, her voice rising so loudly the wolfhound barked and sat back on his haunches.

Noel bent down to rub the dog behind its ears. "Easy, fella. Everything is under control."

Was it? She scooped snow off the fallen log and pressed it against her cheeks. She'd never felt more out of control in her life. She controlled the characters in her books the same way she controlled her life. Emotions were measured. No extremes were allowed. Outcomes evolved after thoughtful consideration and debate.

"Holly, I want to kiss you." Noel's head was still bent toward the wolfhound as he said the words that quickened her heart. He stood slowly and turned to face her. "I've wanted to kiss you from the first moment I saw you at the airport. Everything you shared in your emails rushed back: the love and devotion you have for your family, the way you care about people, and how you never take the writing process for granted and are always reading books on writing or attending workshops. It hit me like a two-ton truck and took all the strength I possessed to resist pulling you into my arms and kissing you in front of everyone. But if you don't feel the same, I'll back off."

Her heart thundered in her chest as she buttoned his shirt. Her fingers lingered against his warm skin and her gaze lifted to his. "I don't want you to back off." She was playing with fire. Where could this go? True, she was crazy attracted to Noel, but she planned to return home after the holidays. "One kiss. But you have to keep your shirt on."

"What about my pants?"

She tried to glare at him and failed miserably when she was forced to press her lips together to keep from laughing. "Yes, you must keep all your clothes on."

"Killjoy. I accept your terms." He swept his arm around her waist, his hand pressing against the small of her back as he drew her against him. With his free hand he cupped the back of her head and lowered himself toward her.

His mouth was warm and tender as he explored, kissing the base of her neck, behind her ears...her eyelids. Each kiss shimmered through her as she ached for more.

When he kissed her on the lips she moaned and pulled him closer.

Chapter Twenty-Five

One kiss had led to another. Holly still felt dazed and out of breath as she walked beside Noel toward the manor in companionable silence. His wolfhound gone off into the woods, obviously bored with no one paying attention to him. Somehow, they'd managed to stop, keep their clothes on, and still pick out the perfect tree and cut it down. They'd chosen too big a tree to carry back on their own, so Noel had called ahead to Jarvis, who promised to get a truck and men to haul it back to the manor. All normal stuff.

Except things were far from normal.

Clouds rolled in, heavy and filled with snow. One moment the day held the brilliance of a winter sun, and the next the sky darkened to the shade of the swords she described in her historical romance novels. The weather here intensified and shifted like her emotions regarding Noel. Before arriving, their friendship had grown over the course of the year and was solid. She'd never considered it was anything more. Their friendship was like August in Seattle: you expected to wake up to a warm, summer day.

But the friendship she felt had changed; she was falling in love with Noel.

They had a mutual respect for each other's talent and work ethic. He'd admitted that, when he first saw her at the airport, he'd wanted to kiss her.

Remembering her reaction to him caused her body temperature to rise. She pulled the scarf over her neck to hide the heated blush. She'd wanted to do more than kiss Noel. She'd wanted to rip off his clothes.

The circular drive and manor looked welcoming as they drew near. It was an idyllic setting for the return of lovers.

Lovers.

Her heartbeat picked up.

Not yet.

Too soon.

Why not?

Why not, indeed. She slid closer to Noel as he talked about his plans for the estate and an idea of offering the manor as a writer's retreat for authors. He and Holly would teach classes and they'd bring in guest speakers, representing agents, publishers, and bestselling authors. The picture he painted felt so real she almost believed it could come true.

The wolfhound had returned to them, and his bark broke the spell as a black sedan pulled into the drive and a woman got out.

Noel stopped short. "Catherine has returned."

****

Holly found a cozy place in the manor that was as far away from Noel and Catherine as she could find. The place looked like it had once been used as a game room. The tops of the tables had inlaid chessboard designs on their surfaces, and a sheet covered a massive pool table. There was a neglected feel about the room. Dust covered the shelves of board games and the tarnished silver chandelier and wall sconces. Quiet games were relegated to the past.

She chose a corner table by a window overlooking a field and set up her workspace. It was a shame about the room. It was large, with great natural light, and would make a perfect classroom for a writer's retreat.

She squeezed her eyes shut, then took a deep breath and opened her computer.

Catherine's appearance as they returned from choosing the tree had been like a bucket of cold water. Holly could make dreams come true in her novels, but real life was a horse of a different color, to paraphrase a line from Shakespeare's *Twelfth Night* and *The Wizard of Oz*.

Holly's fingers poised over her computer's keyboard as she plotted out a new romance. Usually, that was a foolproof way of getting her into a better frame of mind. Writing for her was equal to a spa day for others.

Her fingers flew over the keys.

Her characters would meet, fall in love, and live happily ever after. She set the story in the tropics on an island paradise. There would be a five-star hotel with room service and moonlit strolls along a white sandy beach.

Suddenly, her story took a turn. The skies darkened. Waves rolled back and rose taller than a New York skyscraper. They crested like the claw of a predatory beast and pulled the hero and heroine out to sea where they were swallowed by a great white shark.

Holly moved her chair back from the table. "Good gravy," she said aloud. "That storyline is bat-breath crazy."

"Pardon, miss, do you still want your tea?" Jarvis stood in the doorway with a silver tray, holding a rose-patterned teapot with matching cup and saucer, and a plate of currant scones.

She admired Jarvis' composure. He'd encountered a woman talking to her computer and approached her as calmly as though that was a natural occurrence. She smiled weakly and said, "Sorry for my outburst. What I need is a break from my overactive imagination."

His stoic expression locked in place. "Think nothing of it. Noel often talks to himself when he's writing. If you are looking for a break, I might make a recommendation," Jarvis said as he set the tray down on the table next to Holly's laptop. "Noel's mother used to say that decorating the Christmas tree during the holidays gave her joy and a sense of calm. She loved to travel and collected ornaments from all over the world and would say that using them helped her relive the happier times before she became ill."

Holly powered down her computer. Noel never talked about his mother other than that she'd died of cancer when he was young. Holly had never pressed. It was still difficult for her to talk about her father's death or the type of cancer that killed him. She preferred to remember the way he had lived, not the way he died. But going through the things Noel's mother had collected felt wrong without his permission. She wasn't sure how she would feel if the roles were reversed.

"Jarvis, I love the idea, but not without Noel's permission."

He turned his head to the side. "Extraordinary. You are a very thoughtful person. I do not believe Noel would mind, but in truth, I'm not sure. Noel's father had them packed up and stored soon after she died. He'd planned to sell them but forgot where he'd ordered them placed."

"And you and Clara never told him?"

Jarvis glanced past her toward the window and the fields beyond the manor. "Even before her death, Noel's father was selling off many of the art pieces. It was the topic of many heated disagreements. She wished for everything to be left for Noel, or the money used to renovate the estate or donated to help those in the community. Noel's mother was a generous and kind woman, and when she passed, Clara and I made the decision to honor her wishes as best we could, knowing it might cost us our jobs if discovered. When Noel's father asked if we remembered where the boxes of her ornaments were stored, we said we couldn't remember."

"And he believed you?"

"We may have said the ornaments were of little value and of the mass-produced variety like those sold in the United States."

She frowned at the dig. "What are you saying? We have beautiful ornaments in the States."

"I know that as well. Many of the ornaments Noel's mother collected were from America." He winked. "Noel's father, however, never traveled outside of Europe and believed the United States was still living in colonial times. He bought our story about the ornaments being worthless and stopped asking us to find them. With your permission, I'll take my leave and ask Noel if I may show you his mother's ornament collection."

Chapter Twenty-Six

Noel felt drained. He looked out the drawing room window toward the garden, brown and decayed as it was under the weight of the rain and freezing temperatures. A short distance away, Catherine sat at the table and added sugar to her tea, an indication that she was stressed. In all the years he'd known her, she'd never added sugar to her tea.

"It's worse than I thought," he said.

Her teaspoon clattered against the side of her cup as she added another spoonful and stirred slowly. "I knew it was bad, but Monty told me everything would be all right. He needed to help his friend. Monty valued his friendship with your father and believed, even on the day he died, that your father would repay the loans." She took a sip of her tea and added more sugar. "My Monty was so sweet and trusting. I loved that about him and wished with all my heart we could have a child together. I thought we had more time. Monty was also a man who believed his money would never run out. Even when some of his investments lost money, he didn't worry or consider making adjustments. I reminded him that I had a finance and economics degree and might be able to help. His response was always the same. He told me it was under control and not to worry. I shouldn't have listened."

Noel watched his friend push her tea away and pick

at the red polish on her fingernails. "If the money my father owes is not repaid, how bad is it for you?"

She dropped her hands in her lap. "I think I can manage for a while. I'll have to sell off land, restructure some of the investments, and pray that will be enough. It's a bloody mess, as you English say. But I'm prepared to do whatever is necessary. I've made England my home, and I can't bear the thought of losing the estate and selling off lands that have been in Monty's family for centuries."

Noel joined her at the table, maybe seeing her for the first time. "My father said the reason you wanted to marry was because you wanted a better title than you received married to Lord Montgomery."

She huffed out a very unladylike swear word. "I admit I was obsessed in university about all of that, but now I don't give a toss, as Monty would say." She laughed and shook her head. "Look at me. I'm adopting colloquial English phrases. My sister thinks it cute. My parents, and the relatives from Montana, aren't sure what to think." She grew serious. "The idea of me wanting a better title was your father's idea, and I went along. He was so agitated after Monty's death that I thought it best to keep him calm. My real reason for us to combine our estates is that we might have a chance to save them both."

"We don't have to marry to join forces."

"True, but unless one of us has a sudden increase of capital, our estates are stronger joined in marriage than separate. I'm aware of your plans to make your estate productive again, and I want to do the same with mine. To do that, we will need money, and banks will be more inclined to supply that money if our estates are joined…legally."

"You make a compelling case. Monty should have listened to you when you first told him you could help him."

She took a sip, then another. "Not so bad."

"Neither is your proposal. It is logical."

"I hear an 'except' in your tone."

"Except that we don't love each other."

Chapter Twenty-Seven

Rain mixed with shards of sleet washed against the windows in the drawing room as Noel returned from bidding Catherine farewell. She'd returned to her own estate, leaving him to consider her offer. How many times had he looked out these windows and taken for granted that this would always be his home?

He'd gained more insight into Catherine's motives for wanting to marry and for needing the backbreaking amount of money owed to her estate. He didn't fault her for wanting to find a solution. Upon reflection, she was more generous than most people, given a similar situation. There were those who would have demanded that he sell his home to repay the loans.

Neither could he drop the entirety of this problem at his father's feet. Noel had known his father's spending was out of control and had ignored the signs when Jarvis mentioned his paycheck had bounced. Noel had confronted his father, made sure Jarvis was paid, heard his father's excuses, thought the issue was fixed, and went on about the business of writing. Case closed.

There had been other indications he'd ignored: missing artwork and downsizing of staff. Yet Noel had said nothing and done nothing until it was too late. He was too absorbed in writing books and building his career.

Yes, the blame for the dilemma he faced was on

him.

"Pardon, sir. May I have a word?"

Noel turned from the window. Jarvis stood on the wood-framed threshold between the drawing room and the hallway. As always, the man was dressed in a dark suit, starched white shirt, and a gray pin-striped silk tie. His hair was trimmed and his appearance impeccable. It occurred to Noel that he had known Jarvis all his life and he'd never seen him wear anything but a suit and tie. Jarvis seemed ageless and solid as the stones from which the estate was built.

In the waning light of the day, Noel felt as though he had awakened from a long sleep. Jarvis wasn't ageless. His shoulders were rounded, his eyes less bright, and there had been times in the last few months when Noel had noticed Jarvis limp when he walked. Why hadn't he and Clara retired?

Noel knew of the one time when Jarvis' paycheck bounced. Had there been others? Jarvis and Clara lived on the estate in private quarters, which was part of their compensation. Were Jarvis and Clara still here because they couldn't afford to leave? What would happen to them if Noel were forced to sell the estate?

Jarvis coughed softly and covered his mouth with a rolled hand, a gestured he'd used to gain attention in a crowded room many times before. "Sir?"

Noel smiled, crossing over to Jarvis. "I apologize. Deep in thought, but why so formal? You never call me 'sir.' "

"Perhaps it was because you looked so serious and very much like your grandfather, God rest his soul. He was a good man. He too had dreams of breeding racehorses. He would be proud of you."

It was not the first time Jarvis—or Noel's mother, for that matter—had made the comparison. Noel had never known his grandfather. He'd died before Noel had been born, but stories about him were legendary. It was because of him they had horses on the estate. He had traveled to the Basque region and to the Middle East in search of the best horses he could buy. The mention of his grandfather gave Noel hope again. His grandfather had also faced challenges to the estate with the dangers of two world wars and still managed to survive.

"Thank you for the reminder, Jarvis. Speaking of the horses, I'll check on them before it gets too dark."

"But, sir...Noel. I have a question. Holly wanted to see your mother's ornaments with the thought of using them to decorate the tree that the two of you cut down."

Noel pulled his eyebrows together. "Ornaments? I thought my father got rid of everything connected to Christmas because it reminded him too much of my mother."

Jarvis' eyes lit up in a smile. "Not all."

"You hid them from my father?"

"I did and only wished Clara and I had thought to do more sooner. Your father ordered that we throw out all of your mother's Christmas ornaments. It was the first time in the history of my family's service to yours that we disobeyed a direct order. We went a step further. We knew your father intended to sell the Hemingway ornaments that your mother had purchased before she died, and we hid them as well."

Noel clapped Jarvis on the shoulder. "Well done, and yes, give Holly permission to look through my mother's ornaments and choose any she likes for the tree. Where is this hiding place of yours?"

"In the storeroom behind the manor's chapel."

"The last place my father would look."

"Precisely."

"Let Holly know I'll join her as soon as I check on the horses." The idea of seeing Holly again so soon lightened his mood, and the thought that Christmas was important to her made him smile. Just the thought of her seemed to open the windows and doors to the sunshine.

"And should I have Clara prepare dinner and have it brought to you and Holly in the chapel's storeroom?"

"Excellent idea. As always, Jarvis, you have read my mind."

Chapter Twenty-Eight

A couple of hours later, Noel walked through the chapel toward the storeroom. He wasn't sure how he felt about confronting memories of his mother. Part of him hesitated to revisit the past, while another part of him wanted to face it. This had been one of his mother's favorite places in the manor. Attached to the east wing, the chapel dated back to the sixteenth century and was a smaller-scale version of the Roselyn Chapel in Scotland, or so he'd been told. It had stained-glass windows, stone carvings, and an alcove for a statue of the Virgin Mary.

All of Noel's ancestors had been married in the manor's chapel, including his parents. His father had closed the doors and forbidden future masses to be said after Noel's mother died, believing it would be easier to adjust to her passing if he eliminated all reminders of the things she loved.

Walking through the chapel brought back the times when he and his parents had attended mass here. Those were good memories and made him feel closer to her instead of distant. Not for the first time, he disagreed with his father's decision regarding his mother. Memories were a good thing.

He headed toward the back of the chapel and opened the door to the storeroom. The room was well lit, with a large stained-glass window of a rose garden on the outside wall. He expected dust and cobwebs. The place was as neat and tidy as it must have been when his mother was alive. He knew this was Clara's doing. She and his mother had been friends, and this was Clara's way of honoring her. Boxes were stacked on shelves on one side of the room and on the other was a bank of wardrobes.

He remembered this room and the wardrobes especially. He would come here with his mother while she worked with Clara to sew linens for the church's altar or arranged flowers for feast days and Sunday mass. While they worked, he would play in the wardrobes and pretend that he was Prince Caspian from *The Lion, the Witch, and the Wardrobe*.

Another good memory of his mother.

"Holly, are you still in here?"

"Over by the window, behind the boxes," she shouted back.

Holly sat cross-legged, surrounded by open boxes of an assortment of round red and green ornaments, as well as silver and crystal ornaments shaped like white snowflakes. Holly was smiling and looked like she was having the time of her life. The winter sun filtered through the stained-glass window in shades of pink and yellow light, making Holly's skin glow. The kiss they'd shared in the forest had opened the door to the possibility that happiness was attainable. When Catherine returned, that door had closed and locked.

Catherine made the case that, without an infusion of cash, neither one of them could make the changes necessary to ensure the long-term survival of their estates. Then she'd put the last nail in the coffin, mentioning that, because of the debts attached to his property, obtaining a bank loan would be difficult.

That was an understatement.

He'd already tried and failed. The banks in town hadn't laughed when he applied for a loan, but they might as well have. The message was clear. There was too much debt on his lands to grant a loan. As Catherine had pointed out, their marriage would solve the issue. The realization hit him like a punch to his gut.

Noel joined Holly. She was on the phone.

She unwrapped one of the ornaments from a box on her lap and snapped a picture of it with her phone. She then placed the phone to her ear. "Mom, I sent you another photo." She paused, apparently listening to her mother's response. "Yes, I counted them and there are twenty-five ornaments in the set: one for each of the twenty-four days leading to Christmas and one for the twenty-fifth with a special Christmas wish." She paused again and nodded. "Yes, each one is signed and dated, and I've seen his signature before, so I'm sure it's his, but we'll have to find an expert who can authenticate Hemingway's signature. How long will it take for you to find out how much they could be worth if it is his signature?" She hesitated and blushed a deep rose-pink as she slid Noel a glance. "Yes, Noel does look better than his photo. I love you too," she said as she ended the call.

"You do too, by the way," he said, unwrapping an ornament shaped like a snowman.

She set her phone on the top of a box. "I do too what?"

He wanted to reach out, take her in his arms, and kiss her like he had in the forest when they were searching for a Christmas tree. He wanted to tell her he was falling in love with her. He held back. It wouldn't be right. Not when he was considering Catherine's proposal. He had to tell Holly.

Instead, he answered her question and asked one of his own. "You look much better than your photo. Why were you taking pictures of my mother's ornaments?"

"We have to talk," she said.

Chapter Twenty-Nine

Noel frowned. "Isn't that the opening line someone in a relationship uses, generally followed by the response: 'Are we breaking up?' " Noel picked up one of the tissue-wrapped ornaments, only to set it back into its box without examining it.

Holly started to laugh, then thought better of it. Noel was too serious. Something was wrong. There had been a shift in him. She'd noticed it as soon as he walked into the chapel's storeroom while she was talking to her mom. What had happened between him and Lady Catherine? It was as though a dark cloud hovered over him. He looked bone-weary.

She plunged forward, hoping her news would cheer him up. If she was right, this might solve some of his financial problems. "Jarvis mentioned your mother collected art."

"Which my father sold." There was an equal measure of anger and sadness reflected in Noel's tone.

She scooted closer to him on the floor. She didn't like the emotional distance he'd created between them. "What about ornaments? By any chance did she travel to Europe to purchase them?"

"She and my father never left England. My grandfather knew she was a collector and always brought back ornaments from his travels. My father considered them a waste of money. I'm sure he would have preferred my grandfather had brought back one of the old masters so he could turn around and sell it."

"I'm sure your father had his reasons. Like you, he was trying to help keep the estate. It must have been painful for him to sell the beautiful things your mother collected."

A muscle flexed over his temple as Noel ground out his words. "You don't know, but then, how could you? It's one of those family secrets we English are so good at hiding. My father gambled away what it took our ancestors centuries to accumulate. When he gambled, and ran through our cash, investments, and any art he thought was valuable, he started borrowing money from his friend Lord Montgomery. The only reason my father couldn't gamble away the lands and the manor house was because it was in my name. For some reason, my grandfather put it all in a trust in my name, and my father couldn't touch it. But he managed to get his hands on the money in my mother's accounts, and her jewelry, and her art collection. I didn't find out until it was too late. I was too absorbed in participating in book tours and writers' conferences." He shook his head and fingered the design of a sleigh drawn on a white ornament. "I feel so guilty. I should have known."

She drew closer until they touched. She could feel the pain radiating from him. He blamed himself. She'd also felt guilty when she learned that her mother and stepfather were in danger of losing their home because of medical bills. But people were masters at hiding secrets from those they loved. Life was never black and white. Life was lived in the shades between.

She leaned her head against his shoulder. "I'm so

sorry. You know this is not your fault. And I'm sure your father knows what he did was wrong and it's tearing him up inside with guilt."

Noel took her hand in his. "Do you know that you're the first person who hasn't attacked my father for what he did?"

She covered his hand with hers. "I'm not saying that what your father did wasn't wrong. I'm suggesting that he might need help."

"He told me he is staying in town and plans to meet with a counselor."

"That is a positive first step." She hesitated, trying to figure out the best way to proceed. Then, as though she heard her stepfather's words in her thoughts, she said, "My parents are arriving in the next few days, and my stepfather has been helping people like your father for over twenty years. You don't have to respond. I'm just putting it out there."

He brushed a strand of hair behind her ear. "Thank you. There is so much more to you than I'd imagined." Just as she thought the barrier between them had lifted, it dropped back in place. "Thank you," he said again. "I'm concerned it might be too late for my father to change."

She felt his continual retreat but kept her voice light and her smile in place. "Well, hold onto that thought, because there is more to come. Jarvis kept these ornaments hidden from your father after your mother's death. If I'm right, they are worth a small fortune."

"They're just ornaments."

"These are no ordinary ornaments. There's also a note in the box addressed to your mother." Holly unwrapped aged tissue paper from a red ornament with the image of a snowman in a black hat.

He took the ornament from her hand and turned it over. "Someone has scribbled all over it with a permanent marker. It's ruined. How can you think they are worth anything? Are all of the ornaments like this one?"

"Yes, and at first I also thought that meant they were ruined. Then I looked closer." Feeling her excitement grow, she reached in and selected another ornament and removed its tissue paper. "Prepare to have your mind blown. Spoiler alert: it's a very good thing that Jarvis and Clara hid these ornaments from your father. Most of them are what you'd expect and although beautiful and worth much more than their purchase price, none of them would have been considered priceless. None that is, until I stumbled upon these." She handed Noel the ornament she'd unwrapped. "I almost discarded them at first, thinking your mother had let you scribble on them. Believing that was the case, I was curious about what a boy of about six or eight might have written. Especially since that young man went on to become a writer."

"My mother would never have allowed me to deface one of her ornaments, regardless of their value."

"Good to know, but I'm glad I didn't realize that, because if I hadn't examined them more closely, I might have overlooked their real value." She pointed to the writing on the ornament he held. "Look closer. Do you recognize the line?"

Noel brought the ornament over to the window and read aloud. "How little we know of what there is to know." His glance snapped toward Holly's. "It's a line from the novel *For Whom the Bell Tolls*, written by Ernest Hemingway."

Her smile broadened. She loved that he recognized Hemingway's line. "That's not the best part. Look at the signature. It's on the bottom of the ornament."

His eyes widened. "The signature reads 'Ernest Hemingway.' That can't be right. Is this real?"

"That is what the phone call to my mother was all about. She's taking the photo I sent her of the writing to authenticate the signature. I'm sure they'll need to see the original, but that will at least give us an indication that we're on the right path."

"If it *is* Hemingway's signature…" Noel began, "it could change everything."

She noted the change in him as though a window had opened and let in a ray of light. "Do you want a break? We could go for a walk."

He rewrapped the ornament and set it back in the box gently. "The day is a soggy mess, and it looks like it's going to rain." The sparkle in his eyes sent the message that he'd turned a corner. "Yes, I'd love to go on a walk with you." He pulled her against him, kissing her lightly on the lips. "Thank you."

She settled against him and whispered against his mouth. "We still don't know for sure…"

"But there is hope," he said as he deepened the kiss.

Chapter Thirty

Noel, with Holly's help, had removed all twenty-five ornaments from their cardboard boxes and the aged and disintegrating tissue, and repackaged them in clean tissue paper. He'd then moved them to the entry, beside the Christmas tree he'd chopped down for Holly.

Ernest Hemingway? What were the odds the signature was authentic? And why hadn't he known about the Hemingway ornaments before? The only explanation he could think of was that the ornaments weren't a Christmas gift for his father but for him, and his mother had wanted to keep it a surprise. But there was no way to know for sure.

The telltale clip-clop of high-heeled shoes on the wood entry and the smell of strong, lilac perfume, alerted Noel that Catherine had arrived. He squared his shoulders for the announcement he must make. If the Hemingway signatures were authentic, the sale of the ornaments would likely bring in enough money to pay off the loan to the Montgomery estate. The unknown was how Catherine might react.

She glanced toward him briefly as she entered his line of sight, then paused beside the tree. "You have a Christmas tree," she said, stating the obvious.

Noel nodded. "Holly said it helps cheer up the place. We plan to decorate it later."

"Ah, so it was Holly's idea, and you agreed. I see.

That makes sense." She moved over to the box of ornaments. "Jarvis mentioned that you and Holly had discovered the means to save your estate from bankruptcy. He was quite beside himself. I never knew the man could smile."

"Jarvis only wants what's best for my father and me."

"And I don't? I'm well aware that Jarvis doesn't approve of me. He wants you to marry for love."

"Catherine…" Noel had heard the vulnerability in her voice. Loneliness had drawn them together, but it hadn't been enough. "Don't you want to marry for love?"

"I tried marrying for love the first time around, remember? Everyone believed I married Monty for his money. They forget I had my own money. When he died, it almost destroyed me. I finally understood why your father gambled. He thought it would help him fill up the empty space in his soul. He really is trying to make amends and wants to see you after the holidays."

"My father said he's meeting with a counselor."

"Yes, it's a counselor who helped me…who continues to help me. You have to forgive your father."

"Holly said the same thing to me in one of our emails a while back."

"I knew I liked her, and I really didn't want to. After all, she's my competition."

"It is not a competition."

Catherine gave Noel a kiss on each cheek. "Silly boy, everything is a competition where the heart is involved."

Chapter Thirty-One

It shouldn't bother Holly that Noel was meeting with Lady Catherine.

It shouldn't...but it did.

The next afternoon, after a morning spent switching back and forth between writing scenes for the Amber and Greyeyes novel and editing ones from the book she was writing with Noel, she'd given up when she started confusing the characters' names. This had never happened to her before.

She'd moved from the drawing room to a quiet space with a large picture window that overlooked the stables, hoping that would help clear her mind.

More failure.

The proof that she'd lost her power of concentration was when her couple from the book she was writing with Noel had inexplicably time-traveled to the Wild West of the nineteenth century. She blamed her distraction on realizing that Noel was meeting with Lady Catherine.

The woman seemed to visit every day, and it was getting on Holly's last nerve, so a couple of hours ago, she had given up on writing altogether, switched gears, and moved to the drawing room. Sorting through Christmas decorations from the attic was the perfect solution.

Surrounded by boxes filled with decorations, she'd

been going through the ornaments Jarvis had brought down to the drawing room, deciding which ones to use to decorate the tree she and Noel had chopped down.

As a child, she'd always loved the day her mother brought out the Christmas decorations to unpack. She and her brothers would unwrap each one and share memories of the ones they'd made as children and the ones they'd given each other. So far, she hadn't found any handmade ornaments in the boxes. The Hemingway ornaments might prove to be worth a small fortune, but in her opinion, it was the handmade ones that were most valuable.

She pulled masking tape off a box and looked up as Jarvis entered.

"Pardon the interruption," Jarvis said with a slight bow. "Your family has arrived."

Holly unburied herself from the mounds of tissue she'd flung from the ornament boxes and sprang to her feet. "Thank you so much!" Excited, she swept past Jarvis. "They arrived early," she shouted over her shoulder. "I expected them tomorrow or the day after."

"They were able to take an earlier flight," Jarvis said as she raced past him. "I've sent word to Noel…"

Holly burst from the drawing room and headed down the hallway in the direction of the entry. She hadn't been away from home for long but was anxious to see her family. She'd never been away from home this close to Christmas. She missed them. She guessed going through all the boxes of ornaments was the cause.

She pulled open the double doors of the entry and rushed down the stone steps, slick from the early morning rainstorm. A black taxi was parked in the circular driveway, a short distance from Catherine's red

Mercedes sedan. Her parents were standing beside the taxi while her brother Simon unloaded the luggage.

"Mom, Dad, Simon," Holly shouted, racing down the stairs to embrace them. "I missed you. I can't believe you're actually here."

Simon set down the suitcases and gave Holly a hug. "England agrees with you, sis."

Her mother and stepfather hugged her again, both laughing and telling her how much she was missed as well.

"I'm so glad you all came," Holly said.

"Of course we came," her mother said, kissing Holly on the forehead. "You kept piling on the reasons why we should be here. You gave us no room to refuse. Jasper sends his love. He's holding down the fort back home, and Patrick and his wife also sent their love."

"We only needed the one reason, though, to visit," her stepfather said. "All you had to say was that you needed us. After that, nothing would have kept us away."

Holly's smile widened. She was so grateful to have her family in her life.

"Who are these people?" Catherine said, her voice emphasizing the last word. She stood on the top step in front of the door, shivering from the cold. She wore high-heeled boots, a winter-white short skirt, and a matching silk blouse; she looked every inch the proper country English lady.

"Lady Catherine," Holly said. "I'd like you to meet my family."

"Does Noel know they're here?" she said, marching down the steps like a general confronting her troops.

Holly couldn't understand why Catherine was upset. This wasn't her home. Had her meeting with Noel not gone well and this was her way of deflecting her disappointment?

Catherine slipped and missed the bottom step. Her arms windmilled as she fought to regain her balance.

Simon caught her before she fell and lifted her in his arms. "I have you, Kate."

Catherine looked stunned as her gaze locked onto Simon's. Her arms had gone around his neck as though they'd had a mind of their own. Simon held her as though he would never let her go.

Holly's mother leaned toward Holly and whispered, "Well, isn't that interesting? If you were writing a first meeting between your hero and heroine, would this be called a 'meet cute'?"

"Most definitely."

"What's everyone staring at?" Noel said as he approached Holly.

"I'm not sure," Holly said in a whisper.

"Sure you are," Holly's mother said with a grin. "Your brother just found his match, and from how she's looking at him, she feels the same." Holly's mother held her hand out toward Noel. "Hello, you must be Noel. I'm Holly's mother, Dorothy, and this is my husband, Bill. The one holding Lady Catherine is Holly's brother Simon. Come along, everyone," she said, "we should give these two lovebirds some space."

Chapter Thirty-Two

Holly perched on her mother's bed while her mother unpacked. The whole incident between Lady Catherine and her brother had ended as fast as it began. Lady Catherine had thanked Simon, made a comment that no one had ever called her Kate before, and then had driven away in her car. Simon was equally as quiet, as though nothing out of the ordinary had happened. Holly wondered if she should say something but dismissed the thought. It was probably nothing, and her mother, being the hopeless romantic, had probably overstated the attraction between Simon and Lady Catherine.

Her stepfather had gone for a walk with Simon and Noel, to give Holly some mother-daughter time. "It looks like you had a good flight over," she said, relying on small talk to begin the conversation. "You don't look at all tired."

Her mother hung the last of her clothes in the wardrobe as she removed a stack of Christmas sweaters from her suitcase. "Patrick surprised us and upgraded us to Business Class. It was so luxurious, and I had a nice chat with one of my favorite nonfiction authors in the row next to ours. Your stepdad, Simon, and I had a wonderful meal, and our seats reclined into a bed so we could stretch out and have a nice long nap. I know I'll be tired later today, but while I have the energy, I want to take a closer look at the ornaments and learn more about the auction idea you have and why it's so important."

"Here goes. The reason is clear cut. Noel's father borrowed a lot of money to feed his gambling, and it has to be repaid or Noel will lose his home."

Her mother sank down beside her on the bed. "That is horrible. I'm so sorry, but I'm glad you asked for my help. We'll figure this out." She hesitated. "How is Noel's father doing? I mean, has he sought help?"

Holly fingered the snowflake-shaped buttons on one of the Christmas sweaters in the suitcase. "Noel thinks so." She left the comment dangling.

Her mother squeezed Holly's hand and took another stack of Christmas sweaters from the suitcase. "Don't worry. Your stepdad will know what to do."

"Holly felt a lump form in her throat. She was so grateful her mother and stepfather were here. "Bill is wonderful," she said and received a big smile in response from her mother. Handing her mother a third stack of sweaters, she asked, "How many of these did you bring?"

"Clearly, not enough. I should have brought more. I challenge anyone to ignore the spirit of Christmas when they're wearing a sweater with an embroidered Rudolph the Red-Nosed Reindeer. Noel's home is lovely but in desperate need of decorations. We'll start on that in the morning, and I'll give a few of these sweaters to Jarvis and Clara."

"Mom, you are amazing. By the way, sweaters are called 'jumpers' in England, and I doubt Jarvis will wear one. He's very traditional."

"There is always room for change. You'll see.

Now, let's talk about this auction idea. The old place is stuffed with goodies. You and Noel will have to tell me what's off limits, because I see endless possibilities. My fingers are itching to get to work and start cataloging and writing up descriptions."

Holly loved how her mother wanted to help Noel. "Thank you, that's exactly what I wanted to hear, and Noel will be so grateful. He's skeptical, though, because in addition to borrowing money, Noel's father sold all the valuable art and collectables. He probably would have sold the ornaments if he'd known of their existence."

Her mother picked up a crystal box with a matching lid and held it up to the light by the window. The cut-glass crystal had an amber tone that caught the afternoon sun. "That may be true. What I've discovered, however, is that the people who attend auctions are motivated by the purpose of the auction and how the money will be spent. For example, the most successful auction I helped organize was for the benefit of an inner-city school in Seattle."

Holly sighed and scooted against the headboard on the bed. Maybe her idea wasn't going to work after all. "Noel needs the money to repay the loan. How can we get people excited to spend money on something like that?"

"Hold on. A while back you told me that Noel's family had been part of this community for centuries. That's a start. We can pitch the auction as a way to preserve history."

"Won't we need large ticket items?"

"Not at all," her mother said. "In some cases, it's better to have a variety of affordably priced items than a few art pieces that are out of most people's price range. That way you can attract more people in the community. It all started when one of the first women wartime journalists died and left her estate to the county. Her wish was that the items in her estate be sold and the money used to establish a fund for school supplies, computers, clothes, or whatever was needed to enrich the students' experience in our local school district. She had an eclectic collection of photos, postcards, colorful masks, pottery, as well as bead bracelets and handwoven rugs. We used the title of the song, 'He Has the Whole World in His Hands.' Those who participated had a glimpse into the rich life the journalist had lived through the things she had collected."

"Noel's mother would have loved that auction. He said his mother was more interested in the story behind the item than its worth."

"Smart woman," her mother said. "What you and I will do, then, is create a story and a theme for the auction. If you don't mind, I'll need your help with the descriptions. Those descriptions of the items in Noel's home will tell a story based on the theme we choose. We want people to have fun reading the descriptions. The more fun they have, and the more connected they are to the items, the more they will buy."

"Of course I'll help you, and I think Noel and I stumbled on the perfect theme. We found a journal written in the Victorian era about star-crossed lovers and unrequited love." Holly reached for the crystal box. "With your brilliant strategy in mind, we can write a description of this box and add that it could have been used to hide notes from a lover, or a special keepsake pendant or ring." Holly set the box down and hugged her mother. "I love your idea. This will be fun."

Her mother smiled as she put on a sweater. "I'm glad you like the idea. We might have to ask Patrick if he can change our plane reservations. We're scheduled to return home soon after Christmas."

"No need, unless you want to stay longer. The auction is scheduled for Christmas Eve."

Her mother sank down on the bed. "That is impossible. Christmas is only five days away. There is no way we can get all this ready in time."

Holly sat beside her mother and patted her hand. "We don't have a choice. Soon after Christmas is when Noel has to pay back his father's loan."

Chapter Thirty-Three

Noel flipped on the switch, flooding the white-and-green tiled kitchen in light. Wood-framed windows were latched against the storm, and on the table was an almond coffee cake under a glass dome. Floorboards creaked when he headed toward the cupboards that held the coffee and grinder, and outside tree branches pushed against the window as the wind moaned.

He laughed to himself. He had told Holly he wouldn't be surprised if the mansion had ghosts. Not all his ancestors had been angels. He suspected that given the past five hundred years or so, there could be ghosts looking for a chance to seek revenge or right a wrong.

He ground the coffee beans, making enough for more than one person. He hoped Holly would join him, but it was just as likely that one of her family members experiencing jet lag would come down.

Although he'd agreed that it was okay for Holly to invite her family, he admitted he'd had misgivings on several levels. He was used to having the place almost to himself. His father was gone most of the time or kept to his rooms. Jarvis and Clara also kept to themselves and were so quiet that he was startled whenever they appeared.

They said it was because they used the hidden passageways in the walls so as not to disturb him. Noel tried to talk them out of it, and sometimes they complied, but they said it was a hard habit to break. Jarvis explained it had been the custom for centuries to adhere to the previous owners' demands that those who worked for them be invisible. The nobles didn't want to know about how hard it was to prepare meals, or clean the manor, they just wanted it done as though by magical beings. But when Holly arrived, he realized how isolated he'd become—and how lonely.

While the coffee brewed, Noel lifted the glass dome off the coffee cake that Clara had made. It was dusted with powdered sugar and thinly sliced almonds and made his mouth water. He reached for a plate from the cupboard.

Holly had folded into his life as though she'd been a part of it for years instead of days. And when she'd asked about inviting her parents, his first reaction had been that he would have to share her with her parents. But that reaction vanished when he met them. They were as easy to be around as Holly. He'd forgotten what it was like to have a strong family connection. He hadn't realized how much he missed it.

The windows over the sink slammed open, and a sleet-like rain blew inside and showered water onto the counter and floor.

"I thought the windows were latched," he said aloud, leaning over the sink to secure them. "Ghosts," he said, smiling and reaching for a towel. "Well, you got my attention. Are you out for revenge or just bored with haunting this place and want to chat?"

"Who are you talking to?" Simon said, yawning as he entered the kitchen and set a stack of books on the table. "Is that coffee I smell?"

"Yes. Coffee's almost ready. Help yourself, and

there's almond cake." Noel looked over Simon's books and read the titles aloud. "*Legal Research and Writing, Contracts*, and *Criminal Law*. This looks suspiciously like required reading for a first-year law student."

"Guilty as charged." Simon crossed to pour coffee into a mug and then cut a slice of the cake. "Holly doesn't know yet. I had this bright idea that instead of my family hiring lawyers to negotiate contracts for our business, I could keep it in house and do it myself. But law school is kicking my butt. If I make it through the first year it will be a miracle. Do you mind if I cut another slice of cake?"

"Help yourself. And I've no doubt you'll make it through law school. Holly told me you're one of the smartest people she knows and that it was your idea to diversify by making wine barrels when the lumber business took a hit."

Tree branches scratched against the panes of glass like fingernails, as though asking to come inside. Noel's interest perked up. What if it was a ghost? And what if the ghost needed to contact the living, not because he or she was seeking revenge for their murder, but in order to warn the living regarding something that was about to happen? Sort of like the banshees in Ireland, but unlike those harbingers of death, this ghost warned the living because they hoped to change the outcome.

Noel's imagination simmered to life as he used a well-worn kitchen towel to wipe up the rain pooled on the floor. What if there was a story about a burned-out hit man—or a disgraced detective from Scotland Yard—who bought an old house with the hope of starting a new life? Except a ghost appeared and told him about a crime that was about to happen...

"Noel," Simon said in a raised voice. "Sorry to disturb you, but I can't find cream for my coffee."

Noel shook free of the ghost and the hit man storyline. "I think we're out. I'll check. Were you talking to me earlier?"

Simon finished off his slice of coffee cake and leaned back in his chair. "Yes, but I'm used to it. You had the same look on your face that Holly gets when she's plotting a story. Change of topic and you don't have to answer my question except that Holly is my sister and I'm very protective. What are your intentions?"

The ghost and the hit man storyline faded as Noel joined Simon at the table. Noel didn't mind the question. In fact, he liked that Holly had a protective big brother. But Simon didn't need to worry. The last thing in the world Noel would do was hurt Holly. "We're friends…"

"More than friends," Simon added.

"Yes, more than friends, and I don't know if either of us know where this is headed. It's early days."

Simon pushed his plate to the side. "Hear me out. My first point is that I've seen how she looks at you and recognize the signs. She's falling in love, and this time it looks different. It could be as simple as the fact that you're both writers and have that in common. My second point is that you're engaged to the Lady Catherine."

Noel rubbed the back of his neck. "Why does everyone think I'm engaged?"

Simon sat forward. "Does that mean that you are not engaged?"

"No, I'm not."

156

Simon looked visible relieved. "Then you don't love Lady Catherine?" Simon seemed to hold his breath.

Noel stifled a grin. He recognized the signs. Holly's big brother was falling for Catherine. "Catherine and I were friends and dated a short time in college to see if our friendship could advance to the next level. It never did. When she learned about the loan we owed to her late husband, she proposed an old-fashioned marriage of convenience. I admit it was tempting, but fortunately, there's another solution. Besides, a marriage of convenience wouldn't be fair. She deserves to find love. I remember when we first met. It was our first semester at university. She was from the U.S., and all she could talk about was finding her own personal prince charming."

Simon sat up straighter. "Hold on. Are you telling me Lady Catherine is an American? She has an English accent and behaves as though she was born wearing a tiara."

Noel laughed. "That sounds about right. The English accent and airs are all an act she's perfected. Her last year at university, she came here to visit me, and I introduced her to one of our neighbors, Lord Montgomery. His estate is across the river from ours and four times the size. It has the added feature of a fifteenth-century castle that's been renovated. When they met, Montgomery was a recent widower who was looking for a young wife. Catherine got swept up in the romance of marrying a man with an English title and all the pomp and circumstance that went along with it. Montgomery had all the trappings—private jet, yacht, and a villa in Nice. That may have been what attracted

Catherine to Montgomery, but she grew to love him. Unfortunately, he died in a small plane crash a year ago."

Simon left the table and poured more coffee. "Did they have children?"

Noel shook his head. "She wanted children, but Montgomery wasn't interested. He thought they'd complicate his life. I'd heard he had a change of heart but tragically died before they could get pregnant."

"Do you know where in the States she's from?"

"Actually, I do. Her parents own a small winery in Washington State. She has a younger sister who helps their parents run the winery. She made a joke when she told me the name of the city... That's why I think her story stayed with me. She said the winery was in Walla Walla, a town so nice they named it twice. Have you heard of the town?"

Simon nodded, taking a drink of his coffee. "Our family's lumberyard makes oak wine barrels for a few of the wineries in Walla Walla."

The wind kicked up again, rattling the windowpanes from outside as though trying to get Noel's attention. The sound pulled him away from the conversation, and he had to force himself back. The experience of his mind drifting to a story idea used to happen to him frequently and had annoyed both family and friends in equal measure.

He cleared his throat, recalling the thread of the conversation. Simon had begun with justified brotherly concern. Somewhere in the middle of Simon's questions the focus had shifted to Catherine and involved more than small talk or idle curiosity. The man was attracted to Catherine. It was written all over his face. Catherine was as kind as she was beautiful. But Noel felt he needed to offer advice. If Catherine wasn't interested, Simon would get his heart broken. Simon wasn't the first man to come under her spell. It was Noel's turn to recommend caution where the Lady Catherine was concerned.

"Look, Simon, I may be off base here, but Catherine has a one-track mind when it comes to what she wants out of life. She's embraced the life of the lady of the manor, and all the trappings that come with it."

"But is she happy?" Simon left the table and rinsed off his mug and plate in the sink and put them in the dishwasher. He chuckled. "You've become my big brother, and I hear your warning loud and clear. But you said it yourself that you think Catherine's having second thoughts about what she wants out of life. That's a start."

Chapter Thirty-Four

Later that morning, Holly bumped into Noel as he was headed toward the drawing room to write. She convinced him that a change of scenery might help them with their final scenes. The new setting, and its collection of vintage items, might also convince him of the merits of her mother's idea for the auction.

The location had been Jarvis' idea, and it did not disappoint. Although the top floor of the manor was classified an attic, it shared none of the images associated with the name. Morning light streamed through a window that took up the space of one wall and illuminated a spotless room featuring a bank of wardrobes, vintage furniture, and shelves filled with colorful boxes. This wasn't so much an attic as it was a glimpse into the manor's past.

The wardrobes in the attic were a treasure trove of clothes dating as far back as the Victorian era. Holly felt as though she were a kid in a chocolate candy store. There were dresses in a variety of sizes and styles. There were gowns fit for a fancy ball, with embroidered silks sewn with gold thread, high-waisted fashions from Jane Austen's time, the famous Gibson Girl dresses with their broad shoulders and puffy sleeves, and beaded flapper dresses that had been considered scandalous, in their era, because they were hemmed at the knees instead of covering the ankles.

She and Noel had set up their computers at a table by the window. Holly eyed Noel as he typed. How was it possible that the man seemed to grow more handsome by the day? Was that one of the stages associated with falling in love? There were books and love gurus that touted any number of stages, from three to twelve and beyond. Her mother kept it simple and called it the ABC's of love—Attraction, Beloved, and Commitment —and speculated that Holly was somewhere between stage one and two.

Holly did a mental shake to clear her head as she stared at the blank screen on her computer. She'd written a few paragraphs over the last hour for the ending chapter she was writing with Noel, only to delete them and start again. She knew she had to figure out a compromise between a full-on wedding scene, complete with white dress, bridesmaids, three hundred guests, and the release of white doves at the moment the couple was pronounced husband and wife, and an explosion where the couple dies in a fiery car crash. But she couldn't find one.

"I've hit a wall," Holly confessed. "You're having better luck than I am. What's your secret?"

He looked over the rim of the computer and grinned. "No secret. In fact, you told me you use this technique. When you're stalled on one story, outline or write scenes for another one."

Holly got up from her chair. "You're writing a new story?"

He closed the lid of his computer and chuckled. "I know that look. I'm not ready to share just yet. But it's partially your fault."

"Okay, now you have me curious."

He rose to meet her and tugged on a strand of her hair playfully. "Curiosity is a good look on you. It lights up your eyes. Why don't you tell me the real reason we're in the attic when the manor has dozens of rooms to choose from?"

"What do you think about wearing a costume to the Christmas Auction Ball?"

"I will not dress up like King Henry VIII."

"Good. That wasn't a no. I can't believe your parents and grandparents saved all this," she said, spreading her arms to encompass the room. "These wardrobes look like they're divided into fashion decades instead of the clothes being all jumbled together."

"It was my mother's idea. She worked for years asking for donations, shopping at antique markets and collection fairs. She had the clothes professionally cleaned and categorized them according to the reigns of the king or queen of the time. Her goal was to launch her collection during a traditionally themed Victorian Christmas ball at the manor. Guests could arrive in their own costumes or select ones from her collection to wear for the evening. During the ball she would announce that she was converting the west wing of the manor into a vintage clothing museum that would be free for children." He hesitated. "She died before the invitations were sent out. It was Jarvis and Clara's idea to store them, and as time passed I forgot we'd kept them."

"Your mother had a beautiful idea," Holly said, resting her hand on his arm.

A muscle at his temple throbbed as he looked away. "I wish there was a way to honor her wishes."

"Maybe there is."

"What do you mean?" Noel pulled out a black, double-breasted suit with wide lapels. "I think this was my grandfather's suit. I saw a picture of him wearing one like this in his wedding photo."

"In the U.S., a suit like the one you're holding would have been called a Victory suit during World War II. It was considered patriotic to wear a suit like that one. Because uniforms were made of wool and the parachutes of silk, those natural fibers were in short supply. The result was a number of laws and restrictions on men's and women's clothing regarding how many zippers and buttons could be used and how much fabric. Instead of an all-wool suit, for example, the Victory suit was made from a combination of wool and synthetic fibers and limited in colors. The number of suits a man could own was also limited." She paused. "I apologize for the fashion history lesson. Occupational hazard. I love research and sometimes research random things even if they don't make it into my novels."

"No apologies necessary. You should see the files of research I have on off-shore banking practices, terrorist groups, and international laws regarding extradition."

It felt good to talk about their writing habits. She knew by the haunted look in Noel's eyes that the debts against the manor still weighed heavily on his shoulders. How could they not? There was the slim hope that the Hemingway ornaments and the proceeds from the auction would be the miracle they needed, but neither was a guarantee. That his mother had wanted to convert part of the manor into a potentially money-making enterprise suggested that Noel's family's financial problems were not new.

She opened the jacket Noel was holding to examine the fabric. "Maybe there is a way to make your mother's wishes come true. It could be a lucrative revenue stream for the manor. If we advertised it correctly, it could be of interest not only to the people in the area, but the droves of tourists who visit Derby."

He cocked his eyebrow. "Droves?"

She reached for the suit jacket and held it out toward Noel. "Not at first, perhaps. But I think it's worth a try, and we can announce it at the themed Christmas Auction Ball. Why don't you try on your grandfather's suit for fun?"

Noel returned the suit to the wardrobe. "We're having a themed party? I'm not wearing a costume. A trip to the dentist office for a root canal would be more fun for me than trying on clothes."

"Killjoy. You were probably one of those kids whose idea of dressing in a Halloween costume was to cut holes in a sheet and go as a ghost."

"Hey, I'll have you know that ghost costume was a huge success."

She loved their banter, but most of all she loved that his mood had shifted and was lighter. Holly moved from the wardrobe to a shelf with round boxes covered in fabric that ranged from flower prints to stripes. "Please tell me you're joking?"

He pulled out a uniform from the nineteenth century, complete with a sword and boots. "You got me. My mother tried, but I never saw the point, and she never pressed. Besides, Halloween is not as big a deal in Europe as it is in America. What about you? What was the most elaborate costume you ever wore?"

She opened a tall, round box with a black-and-white striped print. She gasped as she pulled out a black silk top hat. "This is gorgeous, and in such great condition." She set it back gently. "Your mother must have had so much fun discovering all these clothes. I'll bet there's a story in each one. Regarding my most memorable costume, my mother made me the Dorothy costume from the *Wizard of Oz* and a smaller, matching version for my doll. When Halloween was over, I continued to wear the dress every chance I got." She replaced the box and chose another one with a rose print. Inside was a black, wide-brimmed hat decorated with Valentine-red roses and matching ribbons. She walked over to the cheval mirror and tried it on.

"You look…" he said, coming up behind her.

She glanced at his reflection in the mirror and cocked her head. "You hate it." She grinned. "You're right. The roses are too bright and the contrast of the red and black too severe. It makes me look washed out."

"I was going to say that you look beautiful."

"Oh," she said, feeling her face warm under his stare. She set the hat back in its box and reached for another as she rushed on. "When you wear a costume, you know it's not just about pretending to be something you're not. It's more about tapping into that childlike part of you that you've kept hidden. When my nine-year-old self dressed up as Dorothy in the *Wizard of Oz,* I felt like I could do anything. Dorothy was a normal girl. She didn't have superpowers, yet when she was thrust into an impossible situation, she conquered her fears, inspired others, and found her way back home.

Costumes can represent a fantasy or a dream of who you are inside, or who you want to be."

He moved from the mirror's reflection. "I do not want to be a pirate or a comic book character. Sometimes I don't know what I want to be."

"Well, you'd make a sexy pirate." She opened another box and removed a garland of multicolored flowers with long ribbons.

"Pirates are supposed to be scary, not sexy."

"I write and read romance novels, so trust me, pirates can be very sexy. Oh, I love this one." She returned to the mirror. "You're missing the point. And because I look on the sunny side of things, a pirate can represent the adventurous side of a person and a comic book hero reveal the inner wish to protect those they love. I noticed you admiring the uniform."

"It belonged to my great-grandfather. He was one of the first wave of soldiers who volunteered to fight in World War I." Noel rejoined her at the mirror. "The garland suits you."

"It reminds me of what some of the characters wore in Shakespeare's *A Midsummer Night's Dream*. It's whimsical and fun and makes me feel as light as air, as though anything is possible."

He turned her to face him. "You don't need a garland of flowers to bring out those traits. I feel that possibility whenever I'm near you." He fingered a powder-blue silk ribbon that brushed her shoulder. "Why do I feel so many emotions at once? You've made me both doubt and hope at the same time. It's confusing."

She leaned into him and tilted her head toward him. "Confusion is a good thing, Mr. Atteberry."

"That theory flies in the face of all the self-help Yodas out there."

She raised an eyebrow. "Yoda?"

"I said I didn't wear costumes. I never said I wasn't a science fiction and fantasy geek."

"I'm very glad to hear that factoid. And to answer your question, there must be confusion and doubt before there is clarity. Confusion gets our attention, it shouts, it bothers us, and it questions us. When it has our full attention, the process of examining the source of our confusion can begin."

He cupped her face in his hands as he drew her lips to his. "I know the source of my confusion. It's you. And thank you."

She leaned into him, embracing the warmth he radiated. "Why are you thanking me?"

"For believing in me, for wanting to honor my mother's wishes, for bringing sunshine into my life. There is a list, but all I can think about right now is your lips."

His lips brushed hers, and the touch deepened, sweeping her into another world with endless possibilities.

Chapter Thirty-Five

The trip into the town was a family affair once everyone realized that Holly was going on a research mission to search out any clues about the author who wrote *Whispers on a Pillow*. Holly didn't mind the company and decided the place to begin her research was at Mable's café and bookstore. Noel had come along as well and had called ahead and made reservations for a table at Mable's café. He and Catherine had an appointment with her lawyer, and Simon asked if he could tag along, making the case that a reading of the will sounded infinitely more interesting than a cup of tea.

Holly entered the café with her mother and stepfather following closely behind her. The hum of conversation in the crowded café added to the festive atmosphere as Holly headed over toward Mable. She stood guarding a large table in the center of the room.

"Welcome," Mable said in her characteristically cheery voice, a smile lighting her face. "This must be your mother and stepfather, Dorothy and Bill. Noel has told me so much about you. Oh, and before I forget, I confirmed with Noel the book signing you and he have planned for next week. Everyone in town will be there."

Her mother's eyes lit up. "A book signing? We should get you a new dress."

Holly laughed. That was so like her mother, to

want to turn every event into an excuse to improve Holly's wardrobe. "No worries. You made me pack several dresses as though I were going to get invited to Buckingham Palace. We should eat. I'm starved."

"I'm glad you brought your appetite," Mable said, "as I have prepared a special meal in your honor—roast beef, little potatoes, and a Christmas pudding." She stepped aside from the table, and the place settings and decorations drew oohs and ahs from Holly and her family.

The centerpiece was a small, live tree with crystal icicle ornaments and red-and-white candy canes. There were six place settings. Mable mentioned she expected Noel, Catherine, and Simon to join everyone later. The plates, cups and saucers, and serving pieces were gold rimmed with different images of a Victorian Christmas painted on the fine china. There were rosy-cheeked small children, the boys in navy suits and the girls in lace dresses with pink ribbons, all gathered around a tree decorated with real candles, miniature dolls, sailboats, and brightly colored balls. There were families singing Christmas carols, and a large bowl had been painted with a family on a sleigh ride in the snow.

Holly's mother looked so happy at the display of Christmas that Holly half expected her to start levitating.

Dorothy brought both her hands to her chest as though it was difficult to contain her joy. "Oh, Mable," Dorothy said with a smile, "this is all so lovely—the plates, the silverware, the centerpiece..." She touched one of the plates gently as though she thought it might break. "I couldn't bear having food covering these works of art."

Mable laughed. "Many of my customers have the same reaction. I assure you they will be fine. They are sturdier than they look. The china is made right here in Derby by a company that's been around since the eighteenth century. In fact, it is still owned by the same family. They make ornaments and vases as well, and each year they feature a new Christmas pattern for their china. This pattern is at least fifteen years old, and I have enough to serve my café, so I bring out this setting for use during the holidays. Actually, the set was a gift from the owners of the porcelain company. They believed my customers would admire the plates so much they'd ask if they could purchase a set for themselves. They were correct, and as you can see, my old set looks as good as new."

Holly's stepfather rested his hand on his wife's shoulder, and his smile was almost as broad as hers. "Mable, you have made my wife's day happier. We were looking forward to spending Christmas with Holly, and now this. Your hospitality is a gift. Thank you. The only thing that would make it perfect is if Jasper, and Patrick and his wife, could be here with us as well."

Dorothy leaned her head against the hand Bill had placed on her shoulder. "I miss them, and we just saw them a few days ago."

"We are big on families, as you can tell, and not just during the holidays," Holly said to Mable. "My brother and his wife are expecting their first child around the first of the year, and her doctor didn't want her to travel."

"Patrick assured me their baby wouldn't arrive until I returned," Dorothy said with a firm nod. "Oh,

Bill," she said with a sigh, "just think of it! This will be our first grandchild."

He smiled at her with love. "You and I will spoil the little one, my love. I can't wait."

Holly beamed. She was so glad they were here. "We should sit down and enjoy the lunch Mable has prepared for us. Or should we wait for the others?" she said to Mable.

"Please, sit down. Noel called and said they're running late. I can start with tea and homemade bread." Mable swiped at a tear and sniffled.

Dorothy sat down in the chair Bill had pulled out for her. "Mable, is something wrong?"

"These are tears of joy, Dorothy. Nothing warms my heart more than being surrounded by a happy family. Noel wouldn't say so, but it is good for him that you are all here. I noticed a change in him when Holly first arrived, and now with her family here, we can truly have a happy Christmas. Noel mentioned that you'd like to ask me a few research questions?"

Holly nodded and pulled out a folder from her briefcase. "Noel and I discovered this journal and the entries tell the story of a young woman named Madelyn who lived at Mistletoe Manor. She was in love with one of the glassblowers at the local factory in town. Have you heard of the story?"

Mable laced her fingers together across her waist. "I can't say that I have. But I'll do a little research. I love a good romance."

Chapter Thirty-Six

Noel had about an hour before he joined Catherine at the meeting with her solicitor, Reginald Taylor. Noel had learned from Mable that his father had his morning coffee at the Daily Drip.

Watching for traffic, Noel jogged across the street to the coffee shop. It was time he made peace with his father. Being around Holly's family showed him the importance of family. Noel could make the argument that his father hadn't been around when Noel had been a child and should be the one to reach out first, but Noel was no longer a child, and he would not give up on his father.

Noel entered the tidy shop that had once served beer and pizza. The beer taps had been removed, and glazed donuts had replaced the pizza. Instead of wine and liquor, coffee brewed in steel canisters behind a green marble counter.

His father sat in a corner, his back to the rest of the customers as he sipped coffee from a white mug bearing the shop's logo. That was a first. He'd never seen his father drink coffee before.

Noel navigated the tables and pulled up a chair opposite his father. "You're looking good."

His father's expression brightened for a split second, then went gray again. He wrapped his hands around his mug. "My father taught me that appearance was everything. Your life could be falling apart, but your suit had to be cleaned and pressed and your white shirt starched." He took another sip of his coffee as a waitress in a red-checkered uniform with a Christmas wreath pin approached the table.

After placing his order, Noel turned back to his father and unleashed days of pent-up concern. "I'm worried about you, Father. Come home. Where are you staying? Are you eating the right food? Are you…?"

His father held up a hand. "You'd make a good parent. I'm renting a room down the street, and Mable makes sure I eat my vegetables. Satisfied? But how could you be worried about me? I've ruined everything I've touched. You are better off without me." He winced and pinched the ridge above his nose. "What am I doing? I'm doing it again is the answer. My counselor said that negativity breeds more negativity. She has a bunch of sayings like that one. And at first it was annoying. I tried telling her that although I'd stopped gambling, I feared relapse. She used the saying 'one day at time.' "

The waitress returned with Noel's coffee and left to help another customer. Noel noted the change in his father. There was a calmness that hadn't been there in a long time, but underneath the calmness lurked strands of doubt and insecurity. Noel took a drink of the strong coffee. "What was her response to your fear that you'd relapse?"

His father sipped his coffee and made a face like he'd bit into a lemon. "I don't know how you can drink this stuff. It's like drinking water that was used to soak my dirty socks. My counselor said I should try new things, and I thought switching from tea to coffee would be a good start. This is called a mocha, caramel, blah, blah, latté. I can't remember all of it. What I do know is that it is too sweet. I wouldn't be surprised if I contracted diabetes."

"I'm not a physician," Noel said, "but I feel safe saying that you won't develop diabetes from drinking one latté. What is possible, however, is that the Queen could revoke your English citizenship if she found out you'd switched from tea to American-style coffee."

The corners of his father's mouth tilted upward in a smile for the first time since Noel had sat down. "That she might," his father said. "That she might."

Noel rose. "I'll get you a pot of tea and a fresh cup."

His father reached over to Noel's arm. "Sit down, lad. The tea can wait. You asked me a direct question about the counselor, and I deflected it with talk of coffee versus tea. My counselor says that's a common defense mechanism. I used that tactic with your mother whenever she asked me where I'd been. At least this time I realized what I was doing: progress, not perfection, as the counselor says. You asked what she thought when I told her I was afraid I couldn't change and needed help. She said that knowing you need help is a positive step. She's set up a meeting with someone she thinks can help me. The gentleman reached out to her a few days ago to let her know he would be in town. She said he was well-respected, and she was hoping he'd stay past the holidays. I'm meeting with him later today. You've met him. He's Holly's father."

The news was so good Noel had the sudden impulse to reach over and squeeze his father's hand—but resisted. His father hated shows of affection in public. "Father, I'm grateful you're getting the help you need."

His father gave a quick nod. "Early days. Speaking of Holly, this is a small town, and people talk, especially when it comes to the town's most eligible bachelor. How is the relationship between the two of you progressing?"

We're friends and coauthors," Noel said, finishing his coffee and looking around for the waitress. "Holly and her mum believe we can raise enough money with an auction to pay off the loan. Especially since we found the Hemingway ornaments."

His father leaned back in his chair. "Those ornaments must be worth a fortune. Some would even say they are priceless and belong in a museum. I thought they were thrown out along with your mother's Christmas decorations."

"Mother's decorations weren't thrown out, nor were the ornaments. They were hidden. Jarvis said it was the first time he knows of that a member of his family disobeyed a direct order."

"Good man. We should give Jarvis a raise." His father shook his head, chuckling. "Son, it seems I'm not the only one in our family who deflects uncomfortable questions. Your expression when I mentioned Holly's name confirmed the rumors. It's obvious you are smitten with Holly, and it's about time, too. I apologize for trying to force you and Catherine together. You deserve to be happy and in love. You deserve a future."

"That's just it. My future is uncertain."

"It's that bloody loan, isn't it? Don't answer. I know that saving the estate preys on your mind. Sometimes I wish you didn't have that burden.

Mistletoe Manor is a huge responsibility. I don't want you to look back on your life with regret because you didn't make time for the important people in your life."

****

Noel was in a good mood as he met Catherine and Simon at the solicitor's office. The conversation with his father had ended on a positive note, with his father agreeing to move back to the manor tonight. And as soon as this meeting with Reggie Taylor was over, Noel planned to surprise Holly. Noel had taken to heart his father's advice about not living with regret and instead making time for the important people in your life. He'd left word with Mable to delay Holly so that the only option she would have was to return to the manor with him.

Reggie's assistant, a middle-aged man wearing a navy suit and an expression as starched and emotionless as his white shirt, motioned for Noel, Catherine, and Simon to follow him. The meeting started on time. Noel wasn't surprised. Reggie and he had attended university together, and their friends joked that Reggie was like a Swiss watch: always working and always on time.

At the end of the hallway, Reggie's assistant opened the door to a medium-sized office. Bookshelves rendered black with age and decades of polish were filled with law books and flanked the floor-to-ceiling windows, while framed certificates of Reggie's and his father's degrees took up the remaining space. Reggie had joined his father's sole practitioner law firm when he passed the bar, and it had been a smooth transition then to taking over his father's accounts when the time came. Reggie was like his father in appearance, possessing a razor-thin build and close-set dark eyes.

That was where the similarities parted ways. Reggie's father was dedicated to his clients' welfare, whereas it was rumored that Reggie was dedicated to making money.

Reggie pulled out a chair for Catherine, gave a nod to Noel, and frowned toward Simon before settling himself behind a desk that was polished a deep ebony. "Before we begin," Reggie said, opening the single folder on his desk, "I must say for the record, Lady Catherine, that I object to a stranger's presence at our meeting. These proceedings are confidential."

"Reginald," Catherine began, her voice as smooth as the silk blouse she wore, "Simon's a friend. I want him to stay."

Noel hid a smile behind his hand. Catherine knew how to handle Reggie. She always had. Noel's only question was why she wanted Simon to stay.

"I can leave if there is a problem," Simon said in an even tone, but his eyes sparkled with a challenge.

"Nonsense," Catherine said, giving Simon a warm smile. "Reginald doesn't mind."

Clearly, Reggie did mind. His pale complexion flushed in red patches. "As you wish, Lady Catherine. I mentioned at our last meeting that the conditions of the will are clear. Unpaid loans are considered assets, and an estate cannot be settled until all loans are collected. The conditions of the will stipulate that the loan granted to Noel's father must be repaid one year after your late husband's death, which is on January 1, a little over one week away. As executor of the will, I am obligated to adhere to the conditions of your late husband's will."

Catherine fidgeted with the gold clasp on her black clutch purse. "Is there no way out of the conditions of the will? I know Monty intended to update his will regarding the loan but never had the chance. He and Noel's father were best friends. Are you positive the will is as unyielding as you say?"

Simon sat forward. "Kate brings up a valid point. My contracts class professor invited a visiting professor to talk to the class on the procedures of contesting a will. Do you think we have grounds here?"

Reggie sat as still as stone. "There are no grounds to contest the will. Lord Montgomery was of sound mind when he signed the will. There is nothing in writing to suggest that he wanted to change his will. The written word prevails." Reggie closed the folder and laced his hands together. "Your late husband was thinking of your welfare, Lady Catherine. He wanted you cared for and living the life you deserve. He also expressed that you should remarry one day, but I doubt he would have approved the choice of the son of the man who placed his estate in jeopardy. Even if you do marry Noel, the conditions of the will hold firm."

"Reginald, I'm fully aware that my marrying Noel would not have changed the conditions, but at least it would have allowed him to continue to run Mistletoe Manor. Regardless, Noel and I are not getting married."

"I am pleased to learn that you have seen reason. Might I offer a solution that will benefit both you and Noel? There is a large section on the west side of Noel's property that is the envy of countless developers. The estimated worth of this land is more than enough to satisfy the conditions of the loan. This option would also have pleased your late husband. He and I often discussed that Oak Castle and Mistletoe Manor were once part of the same estate and the possibility that they should be once again."

Noel felt shell-shocked. The lands Reggie mentioned were the most valuable on the estate. There was a stream, pasture and farmland, and an expansive forest. Cultivating these lands to their full potential was critical in Noel's plan to revitalize the estate. "Absolutely not," Noel said, grinding out his words. "We have another option. I intend to raise the money I owe Catherine's estate by having an auction to sell some of our art and collectables."

Reggie steepled his fingers. His voice was as dead as his eyes. "Except the contents of the manor were used as collateral for the loan," Reggie said, "and you will need your father's permission to sell them."

Noel stood. "That won't be a problem. We're done here."

Chapter Thirty-Seven

Holly stood outside Mable's café and bookstore. The sun was setting, and it was that glorious in-between time when even the most improbable seemed possible. The more time she spent with Noel and learned about his world, the more she wanted to stay in England.

She loved the Northwest with its snow-capped mountains, lakes, and the ferries that traveled from Puget Sound to the Canadian San Juan Islands. But something was missing. And she didn't know what it was until she stepped off the plane and saw Noel for the first time.

Sometimes back home she couldn't think for all the noise of the freeways, all the people who strove for the bigger house and the faster car. But here the clatter in her thoughts ceased, replaced by calm and a newfound sense of purpose, as though she knew the path she wanted to take as well as the person she wanted on the journey with her. She knew this newfound realization wasn't the result of a place as much as it was of a person. And that person was Noel Atteberry.

She tugged on her gloves against the chill evening air, not quite ready to call for a taxi. The town looked like a movie set for a Jane Austen novel, with its quiet strength and devotion to family and friends, and made her want to linger a little longer. Noel was like this town: strong, resilient, and devoted to those he loved.

Her mother, stepfather, and Noel's father had driven back to the manor together, and her brother and Catherine had taken a separate car to Catherine's estate. Mable suggested Holly stay behind so they could look for additional information regarding the authoress of *Whispers on a Pillow*. Their efforts had produced very little new information, but Mable had said she'd search ship manifests for the time period in case Madelyn had changed her mind and had sailed with Willingsworth after all. Even so, Holly was anxious to share what they'd found.

Anxious was an understatement, and the excuse to talk to Noel about what she'd learned from Mable was just that—an excuse. She wanted to see Noel and spend time alone with him. He hadn't made it for lunch, and Mable hadn't known where he'd gone. Maybe he'd already returned to the manor. Every instinct she possessed said that wasn't true. Noel was still here. He wouldn't leave without her.

A light snow fell, dusted the sidewalks, and added to the snow-packed streets. A black taxicab rolled to a stop at the curb, but she waved it away. Had the meeting with Catherine and her solicitor, Reginald Taylor, gone poorly? Was that the reason Noel might have returned without her? Or was she over-thinking it?

The snowfall increased, accumulating on the parked cars and sidewalks, and still she waited for Noel. This morning he'd said they'd return to the manor together. There had been a promise in his eyes that suggested he wanted to have time with her alone. Since her family had arrived, they had little alone time. She would not miss this opportunity. Had she somehow misunderstood...?

She tried to shift her focus from Noel and concentrate on something else. Her mother and Mable had become instant friends and were planning the auction together. Mable filled her mother in on all the English traditions of a Victorian Christmas, and her mother was exchanging ideas with Mable on the best way to decorate the manor and which rooms would be best suited to hold the silent auction. They both agreed on the grand ballroom because of its mirrors and open spaces. In a stroke of good luck that Holly hoped would turn out well for Noel's father, her stepfather and Noel's father seemed to be getting along.

Holly admitted that all the talking and reminiscing about Christmas was contagious. She could visualize the added decorations her mother and Mable described, the tables displaying Christmas puddings, cakes, and cookies as well as roasted meats, greens, and sweet potatoes. She smiled. She always thought of desserts first. There should be music, maybe a band or a small five- to seven-piece orchestra. She'd ask Noel if he knew of anyone in town. The orchestra would play Christmas songs as well as songs made for dancing. There had to be dancing. She could imagine dancing with Noel and feeling his arms around her as he held her close.

She groaned and blew on her hands again. She hadn't made it five minutes before her thoughts turned back to Noel. This couldn't be happening to her. All the signs screamed that their relationship was doomed. They lived half a world away from each other, and both liked being alone more than they liked being with other people.

She shivered and grabbed her hand-knit wool cap

from her coat pocket and pulled it on her head, leaving her long hair to flow around her shoulders. That last thought about liking to be alone wasn't entirely true. She and Noel liked being with each other; it was other people who were the challenge. So that left the long-distance issue.

Noel wouldn't leave England and his ancestral home, and Holly wouldn't ask him to make that choice. She could leave Seattle. Her family would understand. Then what? Would she appear on Noel's doorstep, baggage in hand, and announce that she was staying…indefinitely? How would he react? And what about the issue with a visa? Currently, she could stay in England for only three months.

The cold seeped through her boots and forced out another shiver. Where was he? Should she call him? She stomped on her feet while she debated if she should make the call or wave over the next taxicab. If it weren't for the cold, she'd wait a little longer. Wanting to dress more femininely, she'd worn a flowing skirt and lacy sweater instead of wool slacks and a tightly knit sweater. Of course, she could go inside the bookstore. That was the practical thing to do. But she didn't want to be practical. She wanted to be that person who took chances.

Maybe it was the atmosphere of the town that cast a spell over her and made her think this way. The soft dusting of snow made everything look as though it were frosted with magic and caught in another time. She half expected to see people dressed in Victorian clothes, shopping along the sidewalks for Christmas presents or laughing with friends. It made her believe that there might be a future for them.

As though conjured from her thoughts, she heard sleigh bells, the haunting melody of "Silent Night," and the clip-clop of horse hooves over the street. Through a light curtain of falling snow emerged two silver-gray horses pulling a red sleigh with green and gold trim. It reminded her of a smaller version of the photos she had seen of Santa's sleigh.

She started to applaud her imagination that was so developed it had created sound effects, when she recognized Noel driving the sleigh through the snow. The vison was like a dream come to life.

She shivered again but not from the cold.

His smile was only for her as he expertly guided the team of horses in her direction. She warmed under his steady gaze, imagining he was a knight riding to rescue his true love from a tower.

He pulled on the reins, and the horses slowed to a stop in front of her. His smile broadened as he said, "Care to join me for a ride?" His voice reminded her of fires on a cold night, strong arms around her waist, and heart-stopping kisses...

"You remembered that I've always wanted to go on a sleigh ride."

"I remembered." He jumped down from the sleigh to help her onboard.

She knew as well as he that she didn't need help, but she waited as his arms went around her waist. He lifted her off the ground as effortlessly as though she were made from snowflakes, and then onto the bench seat made for two.

"I missed you," he said.

She wouldn't remind him that they'd seen each other this morning. She could have seen him an hour ago and felt the same way. Wanting to touch him, she brushed snow from the shoulder of his wool coat. "I missed you, too."

"I'm glad."

He tugged the wool hat over her ears. "You look adorable. Will you be warm enough?" He tucked a green wool blanket over her lap.

"I am now," she said, basking in his compliment. Feeling shy, she arranged the blanket around her legs. "But I'm not sure I needed the blanket." She slid a glance toward Noel as he climbed onboard. "How was your meeting with Catherine and her solicitor?"

He laughed and snapped the reins as the horses trotted toward the edge of town. "Solicitor? I'm impressed you are using the English version of 'lawyer.' Reggie Taylor was his typical unreasonable self. I'd rather not talk about him, if you don't mind. Tonight is for us."

"Tonight is for us," she whispered in response, threading her arm through his as she snuggled closer.

The words cast a spell and combined with the lace-like snowflakes that danced in the air as he leaned over and pressed his mouth against hers. The length of the kiss curled her toes, and the duration made her realize that this was not a casual relationship; this was something else.

****

The clouds cleared, and the moon shone like a single pearl on a bed of black velvet as Holly and Noel reached the outskirts of town. The team of horses tossed their head as though enjoying the outdoors as much as Holly as they pulled the sleigh over the snow-packed road.

Since Noel's kiss, Holly's heart beat so wildly she couldn't speak, and her breath came out in deep sighs that frosted the air with desire. She cuddled next to Noel on the bench seat, wanting to be as close to him as possible. Could he hear the beat of her heart and know she had never felt this way before toward any man? Her senses were alive and tuned into his as though they were one person.

His breathing had also changed and seemed as erotically charged as hers. Noel's profile in the light of the moon looked chiseled by a lover's hand. Her lips ached to kiss his mouth, the line of his jaw, and the cords of his neck. What would it be like to touch his bare skin and feel his caress on hers?

Earlier, she had concentrated on the miles that separated England from America instead of those things Noel did to prove to her that distance shouldn't matter.

She knew he had rented this vintage sleigh for her because he had remembered one of her emails where she wrote about how romantic sleigh rides were and planned to write one into a story. He knew her family was important to her and had welcomed them into his home. She'd wanted a Christmas tree, and he'd chopped down one for her. The list built. He respected her skill as an author and had never qualified it with the statement, "You're a good writer…for a romance novelist."

As the sleigh glided around a bend, Holly leaned her head on Noel's shoulder, and he bent over to place a kiss on her forehead. The gesture felt intimate and natural as he focused on the deserted road ahead that meandered under a canopy of trees.

Their homes were still separated by an ocean and

thousands of miles, but they were together now. She didn't want to dwell on the future anymore. She wanted to live in the present and build a life from that point forward. And she hoped his kiss promised that he wanted her as much as she wanted him.

Feeling bold, she rested her gloved hand on his thigh and felt his muscles flex from her touch. His response sent a quiver of pleasure racing through her body as though lightning had electrified the air.

The horses picked up speed, and Noel chuckled softly, then reined them back down to a walk. "Whoa, boys." He chuckled again and slid a sidelong glance toward Holly. "We'll be home soon."

Home.

Under the velvet night's ceiling of stars, the word took on a new meaning for Holly. Noel had said it as though it was *their* home. The word conjured a future together. A future that included days filled with heart-pounding adventures, and nights devoted to making love, interlaced with cherished moments of coffee and conversation by the fireplace.

"Holly…" He turned toward her, and his voice was as molten as his gaze. "I want to kiss you."

He was asking for more than a kiss, and she knew she longed for that as well.

Time shifted, listening for her answer.

After a few failed attempts at a close relationship with men she had dated, she'd avoided intimacy and blamed the failures on a variety of reasons. She'd blamed herself. She'd blamed her boyfriends. Both, and yet neither, were true. The truth was that she had been looking for a placeholder, someone to escort her to parties or her friends' houses for dinners, not someone she could share her life with on equal terms.

Noel was that person.

Noel had always been that person.

He was her best friend and now she also wanted more.

She shifted toward him as her gaze locked on his. "I want to kiss you, too."

His eyes reflected his desire as he let out his breath and reached for her hand. "Are you sure? I mean, I want to make love to you." His words confirmed what her heart had longed to hear.

She looked up at him, knowing that her heart was in her eyes. "I want to make love to you, too. I have never been more sure of anything in my life."

He brought her hand to his lips and kissed her palm, his breath warm against her skin. "I feel the same. You are more than I deserve, so much so that I fear you will change your mind when we reach the manor. We are about thirty to forty-five minutes away, depending on the weather and the conditions of the roads. If I could get cell service in this bloody forest, I'd call Jarvis and send a helicopter so we could get home faster."

Amused by his very serious and practical British way of analyzing things, she nodded. Holly loved that he felt the same way. She wanted to grab this moment in time and hold on tight. "I won't change my mind." She pressed a kiss on his cheek, loving the light friction of his whiskers against her mouth. The sensation triggered a shiver of arousal deep inside her core. She gasped and kissed him again, brushing her lips over his skin. "You don't have a helicopter."

He pulled her hand down to rest on his thigh. "I

know. I was thinking about speed, and renting a helicopter was the first thing that came to mind."

"Or maybe the horses could grow wings and fly us home." She had infused tenderness in the last word she spoke, and the curve of his lips told her it had resonated with him. That and the fact he hadn't seized on the opportunity to say that winged horses existed only in fantasy novels. She slipped her hand from his grasp and moved it higher up his thigh. His body responded as her own ached with the desire to be caressed, kissed, loved… "Why do we have to wait until we reach the manor?"

His eyebrows knitted together. "Beds. A roaring fire…"

"Uh-huh." Her hand moved higher as she reached up and kissed his neck.

He flinched and dropped the reins. "Beds and fireplaces are highly overrated." He reached for her and crushed his mouth against hers as he pulled her onto his lap.

Sleigh bells chimed as the horses picked up speed, sending music into the crisp air and into her heart.

The spontaneity of Noel's actions took her by surprise. She remembered the last scene in the movie *Bridget Jones' Diary* when Mark Darcy kissed Bridget. Bridget had been surprised at the passion of Mark's kisses, remarking that Englishmen like Mark Darcy didn't kiss like that, and he'd answered with a resounding yes, they did.

She reached around Noel's shoulders to pull closer, straddling his legs, and feeling his heat press through the layers of her clothing. She rocked forward, returning his kiss, matching his passion, matching his rhythm as his arms tightened around her.

This magical night had been created with lovers in mind. A breeze fluttered through the trees, releasing snow that caught the shimmer of the stars, while pine-scented branches brushed against the sides of the sleigh.

Noel drew one of the wool blankets around them, encasing them in a cocoon of warmth as he kissed the base of her neck. His touch sent wild shivers of desire chasing through her as she unbuttoned her coat, inviting him to kiss lower…much lower.

The horses neighed as they increased their gait to a canter. Her heart raced with them as each kiss fanned the growing flames of love higher. Transported to another place, Noel's kisses deepened to a new level of desire as each layer of passion built on the next.

The sleigh lurched forward, breaking Holly's grip in Noel's arms, and sped toward a sharp curve in the road. Noel grabbed the reins as the horses stretched out the length of their stride into a gallop. The sleigh tilted precariously as it rounded the corner.

Holly clung to the railing on the bench seat. "What's wrong with them?"

"I don't know. Something set them off. Slow down," Noel shouted, and pulled on the reins. "What's got into you wankers?" Branches scraped against the sides of the sleigh as the horses plunged forward. Muscles corded along his neck as he yanked on the reins again. "Stop. Now!"

Abruptly, the sleigh came to a halt.

The sudden stop pitched Noel and Holly out of the sleigh and into a snowdrift. The deep snow cushioned her fall as well as Noel's. She lifted her head from where her face had been buried in the fluffy snow. As she looked around, the adrenalin rush from the last wild moments of their sleigh ride subsided. Thankfully, she and Noel were unharmed. But what had spooked the horses?

They returned her glare as though to say, "What?"

Covered in snow, Holly laughed, brushing snow off Noel as he angled to a sitting position. She'd often said she wanted adventure, and surviving a runaway sleigh qualified. She should feel scared. Instead she felt alive and grateful she and Noel were together and unharmed.

"Are you all right?" he said, dusting snow out of Holly's hair. "I don't know what got into the horses."

Feeling impulsive, she winked and placed a kiss on his cheek. "They did us a favor. I like this better than the sleigh's bench seat. But maybe blankets on the ground first?"

He gave her a quizzical expression, then light dawned. "Blankets. Lots of blankets." He rushed to the sleigh and gathered an armful as Holly helped him spread them over the snow.

There was something whimsical, romantic, and playful about spreading blankets over the snow. Logically, it would melt, and it wouldn't be as comfortable as a bed. A sensible person would suggest they wait to make love until they reached the manor. Her face warmed under the image of them naked in his bedroom or hers, arms and legs entwined, and bodies heated with passion. She ducked her head to hide the growing blush on her cheeks and added another blanket. She vowed they'd make love in Noel's bed too when they returned to the manor.

Finished with the task of covering the frozen

ground with blankets, Noel pulled her close. "Now, where were we?" He kissed her behind the ear, sending shivers of delight over her skin.

She took a breath, and then one more to settle her racing heart that heated with anticipation. "I believe I was about to suggest we take off each other's clothes," Holly said.

"Brilliant idea."

Her fingers trembled with excitement as she tugged off his coat and wool shirt, exposing bare chest and rippling abs. She sucked in her breath and ran her fingers over his warm skin. Stars twinkled through the woods like Victorian fairy lights placed on hundreds of Christmas trees. She was glad they were alone in the middle of the forest instead of in the manor. She'd always thought an island paradise the perfect setting for lovers. A forest covered in snow and the velvet softness of night replaced that vision.

"My turn," he said, his voice thick with emotion. When she nodded, he removed her coat and pulled her sweater over her head. His eyes smoldered with desire. "Your brassiere is red. That is officially my favorite color."

Her teeth chattered as a soft breeze teased the air. "Maybe I was thinking ahead. And why does the word 'brassiere' sound naughtier than 'bra'?"

"We Brits know the words that evoke an image." He frowned. "You're cold. This was a bad idea."

She drew a blanket over her shoulders and moved closer until her breasts pressed lightly against the hair on his chest. Her nipples puckered in response as her breath caught. "There is nowhere else I'd rather be than here with you."

He said her name in a whisper, like a love sonnet recited beneath a balcony. "There is nowhere else I'd rather be than here with you," he said, repeating her words.

Snow fell around them in swirls of white mist, laced with the silver light of the moon. Noel glanced toward the sky. "I have an idea." He pulled one of the blankets from the pile and draped it over a low hanging branch, creating a makeshift tent over Holly. Once it was secure, he joined her under its cozy warmth. "I'm yours to command."

"Delicious idea," she said against his lips. She unbuttoned his jeans, taking her time, feeling him grow beneath her touch as she eased his jeans over his hips. Her heart thundered in her chest as heat pulsed in her veins. "You're not wearing underwear…"

"Too confining," he said, with a smile against her lips. Shedding his jeans, he stretched out on the blankets and drew her beside him. Removing her bra, his hand rested beneath her breast as his thumb teased her nipple. His head bent lower, kissing the base of her neck and the delicate skin between her breasts, then rolled his tongue around her nipple. "Are you wearing knickers under that pretty skirt?" His breath was hot against her skin, as he rested his hand below her waist.

"Oh, my…" She couldn't think. But she had to get naked. She unfastened her skirt and scooted it down. "Knickers? Oh, you mean panties. Yes, pretty lace ones."

"Not for long." Noel hooked his fingers on the top of her silk panties and pulled them down slowly. Then his hand returned to linger in the place her panties had been. He lightly caressed her, stroked her, and explored, slowly, deeply…

She arched toward his touch as he rolled to take her in his arms.

Branches shuddered and a gentle wind sighed.

Her body on fire, she moaned. "Now," she gasped against his mouth. "Now."

He entered her, and for the first time in her life she didn't care about the future. There was only his touch and the heat of his breath against her skin that mattered. The world fell away under the shimmering glow of moonlight and whispered promises.

Chapter Thirty-Eight

Under the same moon that smiled down on Noel
and Holly, Reginald Taylor, Lady Catherine's solicitor,
stood at the entry doors to Mistletoe Manor. He had
been standing there for the past ten minutes, rehearsing
the strategy for when he met with Noel's father, but
time was running out. He had lost precious time when
he'd been forced to change out of his muddy clothes in
Noel's barn. Thankfully, he'd had the foresight to bring
along a change of clothes. It would not do to meet with
the lord of Mistletoe Manor looking like a common
laborer.

Reginald had dressed to impress, as the Americans
would say, in his finest cashmere overcoat and
matching steel-gray suit. His shirt was starched to
perfection, and his black and burgundy necktie was
made of silk. In his haste to arrive before Noel,
Reginald had forgotten to bring spare shoes and had
only noticed the mud on the soles when he arrived at
the manor. He had remedied the problem by removing
the mud on the cast iron boot scraper by the door at the
entry, and then shining his shoes with his handkerchief
until he could see his reflection.

He had one chance, and he had to do it before Noel
and Holly returned from town. He had made sure their
trip would be delayed in the forest, thus buying him
time. He had given his associate detailed instructions

and marked the tree Reginald wanted chopped down. His regret was that there wasn't time for him to stay and help his associate or, more importantly, to see Noel's reaction.

But enough reminiscing. The longer he stood out here in the cold shadow of the manor, the more likely it was that Noel would return and spoil everything.

He raised his hand and used the brass lion's head door knocker to announce his arrival. The moon glowered down on him as snow swirled around his polished leather shoes. He resisted the impulse to lean down and brush the snow from his wingtips. He couldn't risk being caught bending down when the butler arrived at the door. His father had lectured him that a gentleman must always maintain a casual air of indifference. The mark of the very rich, his father would say, was maintaining the illusion that anything they owned could be replaced. And if it looked like he cared that his shoes were soiled, he risked shattering that illusion.

The door opened, sending out a blast of warm air. The butler stood like a sentinel guarding a castle.

"Mr. Taylor," Jarvis said, opening the door to Mistletoe Manor. "Master Noel and the Lady Catherine are not here. Were they expecting you?"

Reginald handed Jarvis his coat and hat, annoyed with Jarvis. The man didn't know his place. Whether or not Reginald was expected was none of Jarvis' business. "I am here to meet with Lord Atteberry. I am told he returned this afternoon with Holly Lane's parents."

"Lord Atteberry is in the drawing room. Shall I announce you?"

"I know the way," Reginald said with an even tone.

Reginald had thought he had everything under control after Lady Catherine's husband died. Reginald's father had represented Lady Catherine and her husband's estate, and upon his retirement, Reginald had taken over the account and had the perfect excuse to offer support and guidance to Lady Catherine. It had surprised him that she grieved over the lord's death and seemed to have cared for the man despite their age difference.

He had known about the loans Lord Montgomery made to Noel's father and had been the one to suggest the conditions of the loan repayment in the will. It was then he had seen the opportunity. The Montgomery and Atteberry estates had once been united and could be again. Centuries ago, his ancestor had the chance to marry into that family and had given it up for love and poverty. The family legend was that she was happy and content in her choice. How could she be? She had given up a castle for a modest home in town.

The lord had not been in the best of health, but Reginald had expected there would be more time to renew his friendship with Lady Catherine, but the old man had died suddenly in a plane crash. Reginald's plan was to marry her on the lord's death and work to reclaim what should have been his birthright. His goals to woo Lady Catherine had been progressing well until she grew a conscience and proposed the idea of marrying Noel to save his estate. She had backed away from that plan now, believing Noel had found a way to repay the loans.

It was a long shot, and most people would have speculated that Noel could not succeed. Except

Reginald had known Noel all his life, and if there was one thing about Noel that was consistent, it was that once Noel set his sights on a target, he never missed.

Something must be done.

Reginald opened the doors to the drawing room. Lord Atteberry was engaged in conversation with a man of about his same age. From the description Mable had given him, Reginald surmised the man was Holly's father.

When Reginald entered, the lord looked over at him. "Mr. Taylor, this is unexpected. My son has not returned, and I don't expect Lady Catherine until later. She is showing Bill's son her estate."

Reginald felt the blood in his veins run cold as he fought to keep his composure. It was so like Lord Atteberry not to introduce him to the person sitting next to him. Reginald ignored the slight. That was minor to his larger concern. He had seen how Lady Catherine looked at Simon and how she had demanded the insufferable man stay with her at the meeting this morning. First Reginald had learned that it was Holly who came up with the idea of an auction that would raise money to repay the loan, and next Holly's brother was courting Lady Catherine, the woman Reginald planned to marry. Holly Lane and her family were proving to be a thorn in his side. The sooner they left, the better.

Reginald adjusted his tie. "Lord Atteberry, I am here to see you. Alone. It is of the utmost importance. There is something I would like to discuss that might be of financial interest to you."

Chapter Thirty-Nine

The horse-drawn sleigh moved over the snow-packed road and through the crisp air as though enchanted. The snow had stopped but not before it left an accumulation on the Douglas firs and the pine trees, adding to the feeling that she and Noel had entered a magical realm.

In Holly's opinion, she and Noel were headed back to the manor in the most romantic way imaginable. The weather had cleared, and stars frosted the night sky to help light the way.

Her lap covered in a layer of blankets, Holly leaned against Noel's shoulder, floating in the afterglow of their lovemaking. She'd always thought couples needed to talk nonstop, as though proving to the world that conversation was the key to a successful relationship. She was learning relationships were more than conversation. It was feeling safe and secure in each other's presence that built a lasting connection.

"Penny for your thoughts," Noel said above the muffled clip-clop sound of the horses' hooves over the packed snow.

"Would it be strange if I said that I'm enjoying the magic of the evening and allowing my mind to wander?"

"Not strange at all," he said, moving the reins to his right hand so he could put his left arm around

Holly's shoulder.

She snuggled against his warm body. "I suppose we should talk about our characters."

"Oh, them," Noel said with a smile in his voice. "There are times when I'd like to leave them on a deserted island, since you won't let me blow them up."

"At least on an island there'd be a chance for a sequel," she pointed out.

He lifted his arm from Holly's shoulder to take both reins so he could have better control of the horses. "What's wrong, boys? Did you see something in the road ahead?"

"Is something the matter?"

"Probably nothing. They've been acting skittish ever since the road narrowed a while back. Most likely they were startled by a deer or squirrels." He draped his arm around her shoulder again. "Now, back to the ending of our story. What do you think about the deserted island plotline?"

She loved the idea, as her imagination kicked into high gear. She envisioned being stranded on a tropical island paradise with Noel. But she wasn't one of those survivalists who could live off bugs and build shelters out of palm leaves, only to have their home destroyed by windstorms. She didn't need a five-star hotel, but a few creature comforts, and the assurance that they wouldn't be attacked in their sleep by tigers would be nice.

"I like the idea of an island setting for our last chapter." She paused, catching a gleam in his eye. "I know that look. You have a violent ending planned for our characters—a volcanic explosion, perhaps?"

He sawed on the reins to guide the horses around a

wide bend in the road. "Good idea, except you've outlawed explosions."

She enjoyed the comfortable banter and the exchange of ideas. This was how it had been when they first started working together. She especially loved the way his gaze sought hers. "How about this idea? The climax in the last chapter is more of a natural disaster rather than an explosion. Like the Kilauea volcano eruption on Hawaii. We'd write a series of events where our characters run from the bubbling lava and fireballs erupting from the volcano. As tension builds, their escape blocked at every turn, they reach the shore and find a boat."

"Or they could die in the eruption."

She rolled her eyes. "You have a one-track mind."

He grinned and snapped the reins again. "What can I say? My readers love it when I blow things up."

"And my readers love it when my characters kiss and live happily ever after. I think it's because life isn't always kind, and escaping into worlds that hold endless possibilities makes people feel hopeful."

"Okay, that's not such a bad thing." He pulled her closer as the smooth glide of the sleigh's runners propelled them forward.

She sighed, wanting this night to go on forever. Her own life hadn't produced the soulmate sort of relationships she wrote about, and up until now it hadn't bothered her that much. She'd always believed her one true love was around the corner, waiting to sweep her off her feet. Could it be that Noel had been there all along, tucked neatly in the "friend zone"?

Obviously, they'd evolved from that zone and taken their relationship to a new level of intimacy. After making love, shouldn't they be on the same page when it came to the fate of their characters? What was she missing?

A gust of wind blew through the overhead branches and showered down a light dusting of snow. She brushed the snow off Noel's shoulder, then hers, and pulled her scarf up to her chin and sank into its warmth. "I'm worried about our characters." Holly wanted to add that she was also worried about herself and Noel. "We threw our characters together, surrounded them with people who wanted to kill them, and sent them to exotic locations to solve the plot. I've heard relationships based on intense experiences never work."

He released a deep-throated laugh. "That's a direct quote from the movie *Speed*, with Keanu Reeves and Sandra Bullock. Keanu said that to Sandra at the end of the movie."

She squirmed in her seat. "Okay, I hadn't expected you to have seen the movie."

His grin widened. "And what did Sandra say in response?"

"We'll have to base our relationship on sex."

His smile looked self-satisfied. "Not a bad plan."

She frowned. "That is a terrible plan. But maybe your instincts were right all along. I wouldn't want to go so far as to kill them, but maybe they don't belong together. They are from different worlds—he's an international spy and she's a grammar school teacher who's afraid of heights and bats. Maybe at the end of the story they should go their separate ways."

The lead horse tossed his head, jingling the bells on his harness. Noel sat forward. "I'm worried. The horses are behaving strangely. There's a place up ahead where the road widens. I'm going to give the team a break. Are you okay if we delay our return?"

When she nodded, he continued.

"I have the distinct feeling," he said, "that your comment has very little to do with our characters and everything to do with us. I'll let that go for the moment. Regarding our characters, we established why they are attracted to each other. That's in the first chapters. Mr. International Spy brings his nephew to the school where our heroine works because his brother's wife is going into labor with their second child. Our hero notices our heroine's kindness as a second-grade teacher, and she notices how patient our hero is with his nephew. We continued to build on that first meeting, and our characters fall in love."

"Fine," she said, shivering. The crisp air had taken a turn from invigorating to biting cold. "But can you at least admit that we wrote some pretty intense life-and-death scenes where our characters were forced to work together in dangerous situations? Did they really fall in love, or was it the adrenaline rush that was the cause of their passion? What happens when they solve the murder mystery and the story ends? I started thinking about that when Mable and I talked about the two people in the journal we found. Their romance is similar. In Victorian times, a love like theirs was forbidden, and that in itself might have been a turn-on. Then reality hit when the hero asked the heroine to run away with him to the Americas."

"She stayed at the manor, then?" he said as his eyes narrowed on the road ahead.

Holly looked down at her gloved hands resting in

her lap and nodded. "Mable didn't know what happened for sure. She said one version she heard from gossip was that the heroine stayed and never married, and another version was that she left with the hero for the Americas. Mable said she would research more closely on the ship records around that time." Holly paused. "Back to my original concern. If you think our characters are so great, why are you resisting them living happily ever after?"

He pulled his cap farther down on his forehead. "The hero is attracted to the heroine. That's not in question. It's his life story. It's a mess. He goes from one crisis to another with no end in sight. It's difficult for me to see him in a long-term relationship."

She swallowed and kept her gaze locked on his as her pulse raced. He'd skirted around the question, but then she was also using their characters in a thinly veiled way to discuss the budding relationship between herself and Noel. "It sounds like you're talking about yourself."

He snapped the reins, and the horses increased their gait toward the clearing. "I don't have a crystal ball. What I do know is that I care about you, and since it's normally rain or snow falling around us and not bullets, I know that the only adrenaline rush I feel is when you glance at me with those beautiful eyes. Can't we just enjoy the time we have together?"

It was not the answer she wanted, but it was honest. In truth, she wasn't sure about the depth of her feelings either. But because she knew if she spoke her voice would tremble, she nodded and forced a smile.

Chapter Forty

The sleigh came to a stop in the center of a circular clearing as a pearl-like glow shone down from the moon. Noel held the reins in his hands loosely. He would give the horses a short rest before continuing. He knew he hadn't handled his conversation with Holly well. He'd meant to ease her mind regarding the two of them and had only made it worse.

He was sending her mixed messages. She was a smart woman. She knew he was working out his commitment issues through his character, and he had a feeling that she was as well. The irony was that he thought the international spy character he'd created was a fool when it came to relationships. The man was in a rut with no clear path out. The glamorous lifestyle looked good in print, but it was surface stuff without any real substance or balance.

And like his character, he'd kept his emotions guarded for so long that the thought of changing course or letting someone too close was scarier than facing a herd of stampeding horses in the dead of night.

"You never told me about your meeting between Catherine and Reginald Taylor," Holly said. Her breath frosted the cold air as she spoke. "Or would you rather not talk about it?"

He suspected Holly was looking for a neutral topic because discussing their characters right now was like a minefield. He welcomed the distraction. "I don't mind talking about the meeting. Some parts of it were funny. For example, Reggie didn't like your brother being at the meeting. He liked it even less when Catherine told him she wanted Simon to stay. I'd forgotten that Reggie liked Catherine when we all attended university together. She made it clear she wasn't interested, but I don't think he's ever gotten over his crush or ever given up the idea that she'll change her mind. It was obvious that he viewed Simon as a rival."

The wind picked up, rustling through the trees and lifting snow from the branches as the temperature dropped. Holly tucked her hands under the blankets draped over her lap. "How did my brother react when Catherine asked him to stay? He loathes sitting still."

"Your brother didn't seem to mind. In fact, he asked great questions, which only agitated Reggie more. It was fun to watch."

"Well, well, as my mother would say. There's only one reason why Simon would sit through a meeting. I think my brother is interested in Catherine. How did the meeting end?"

Noel jumped down from the sleigh and retrieved a blanket for the horses. He'd give the team a few more minutes before resuming their journey to the manor. "We told Reggie about the auction," Noel said over his shoulder as he secured the blankets. "Reggie brought up ancient history about Oak Castle and Mistletoe Manor once being one estate. He suggested that I just turn over my property to Catherine. I told Reggie that was not going to happen and explained your plans for the auction and the discovery of the Hemingway ornaments."

Holly blew on her gloved hands. "Reggie must have been pleased you have a plan to repay the loan."

"With Reggie, it's hard to tell. But he carried on about the ancient history of the two estates. We're talking eleventh or twelfth century, with a feud involved between brothers who were in love with the same woman. The battle between them went on for years until the king stepped in and divided the holdings between the brothers. Reggie seemed obsessed with the idea that the properties should be joined again."

Holly scooted near the edge of the bench seat as Noel helped her down. "I love this part. It sounds like a historical romance. My weakness. What happened to the woman?"

"She ran off with someone else," Noel said absently, drawn toward a rustling sound that caught his attention. Two roads led from the clearing. One toward his manor and another toward Catherine's estate. "Did you hear something? I thought I heard a humming sound, like a chainsaw."

He gazed toward the road that led to the manor. A deer bounded into view, paused, then leapt in the opposite direction. Branches shuddered, cracked, and snow lifted from the trees. A loud boom shattered the quiet as something crashed to the ground. He knew that sound. A tree had fallen, and by the sound, the tree was large. But there was no wind of any consequence, so what had caused it to fall? He didn't like the suspicious thoughts beating in his head. Was there an intruder in the woods?

"Stay here," he said.

She perched her hands on her hips. "Are you seriously saying that it's safer if you go on ahead while

I stay behind, knowing that is the plotline for almost every horror and thriller movie made these days?" Her voice took on a steel-like tone as she faced him. "And what happens to the person left behind? Dead. Dead. Dead. Or kidnapped and then dead. I am going with you, end of discussion."

The fire and passion in her voice were intoxicating. He couldn't resist. He leaned over and kissed her.

"What was that for?" she said, touching her gloved fingers to her mouth.

"I like how your mind works. But just in case, stay close behind me?"

"I won't leave you," she said.

He kissed Holly on the cheek and felt her smile. He liked kissing her, and after the course of a few days, it felt natural. She was easy to be with, and he was grateful she had wanted to come with him. That was the smart move.

Chapter Forty-One

The clouds rolled in again, blanketing the night as black as the inside of a mountain cave. Noel found a flashlight in the compartment under the bench seat and, with Holly's help, secured the horses while they investigated. The horses had quieted, and he hoped that was a good sign that whatever or whoever had them spooked had left.

Had he imagined the humming sound a chainsaw made? He must have. His imagination was in free fall. Forget the whole "private property" aspect. No one in their right mind would cut down a tree in the dead of night.

Holly had pasted on a brave face and helped him quiet the horses. He had expected her to collapse in a hysterical puddle, but she hadn't. Still, he wouldn't have blamed her if she had. He was a little freaked out, if he was being honest.

There could be an easy explanation. Trees uprooted and fell in the woods all the time, either from increased rain, or diseases and fungus that weakened their root system. That didn't explain the sound of a chainsaw.

He reached for Holly's hand and trained the flashlight on the road that led to the manor. The canopy of branches dipped lower than they had a few days ago; understandable, he reasoned, with the amount of snow that had fallen.

Even with the miserly glow from the moon and the dark shadows, the road looked more overgrown than it had the night he returned with the colt he'd rescued from the rain-swollen stream.

"Are you worried the tree that fell is blocking the road?" Holly said in a whisper.

The fact that she was whispering told him she thought something wasn't right either. He wouldn't lie to her. "I've spent a lot of time outside and know these woods, roads, and trails better than the rooms in the manor, and something feels off."

Holly tightened her grip on his hand, keeping whatever thoughts she had to herself.

Noel ventured farther down the road with the flashlight trained at shoulder level. Holly, a woman of her word, walked beside him, glued to his side. The only indication of her concern was that she'd looped both arms around his. He was glad she was with him. If something was out there, he wanted her close where he could protect her.

He clenched his jaw against all the possibilities that scrolled through his head. He was allowing his author's imagination to run amok, although he was probably overreacting.

Then he saw the tree.

The flashlight illuminated a wall of thick branches. A large tree, with reddish-brown bark, had fallen across the road. Noel shone the beam from left to right, then straight up to gauge the height. He and Holly could climb over the tree, but it was too heavy to move by themselves and too cold to leave the horses behind while they walked to the manor.

She reached out toward the tree, touching its soft

needles. "This is a Douglas Fir, named after the Scottish botanist David Douglas, who brought seeds from America to England in eighteen twenty-seven." She paused, smiling and shaking her head. "Sorry for the history lesson. I researched these trees for a book. We have Douglas firs in the Northwest, and they are very hardy, with wide root systems." Her light conversation shifted as her voice shook. "They rarely blow down."

Noel registered what Holly said, and it sent a chill through his bones. He had been right about the chainsaw. He motioned for Holly to follow him and dove into the brush.

"What are we looking for?" she said, her voice raised.

"I'll know it when I see it."

He didn't have to go far.

He reached the base and knelt. There was a clean cut three quarters of the way through the trunk of the tree. The thick umbrella of branches had protected the floor of the forest from snow but not from the rain. The ground was soft and muddy and there were two sets of footprints. One looked like boot prints and the other like dress shoes.

Holly leaned over his shoulder and sucked in her breath. She'd seen the same thing he had. The tree had been chopped down—but why?

Noel's thoughts raced into dangerous territory. He didn't want to panic her. He was panicked enough for both of them. He didn't like the coincidence of a tree falling on the exact road they were taking.

"Could be an accident." He tried out his theory out loud. "Someone came into these woods to chop down a tree for firewood. It got dark and they left, planning to return in the morning." The words sounded hollow in his ears. These were his lands. Anyone caught cutting down a tree without his permission would have been fined. And no one had asked him for permission. This was something else.

"You don't believe this was an accident," Holly said, her voice trembling.

"No, I do not." He motioned for her to follow him back to the road and the clearing where they'd left the sleigh and horses. "The tree is too large to move by ourselves. We'll have to take the long way around to reach the manor."

Holly had taken out her phone and was holding it up toward the sky. "No cell service. We could go back to town. I'm sure Mable will help us find a place to stay."

Under the circumstances, he didn't like the idea of traveling in the woods this late at night any more than she did. "It would take longer to retrace our steps to town than to take the detour to the manor."

When they reached the clearing, he removed the blankets from the horses and climbed in beside Holly. "Still like sleigh rides?"

Chapter Forty-Two

The welcome warmth of the entry greeted Holly as she and Noel entered the manor. It had been a long night. They'd taken the detour route to the manor, and although she felt safe riding beside Noel, what had begun as a romantic sleigh ride in the snow had turned suspenseful and scary after the road was blocked. They'd had a somber discussion around the mystery of who had cut down the tree, without a clear outcome.

But the closer they came to the manor, the more distant Noel had grown, despite her attempts at humor, suggesting their mystery woodsman was a version of the Northwest Big Foot. Now that they had returned, she was hopeful they'd discover a reasonable explanation for the tree.

Jarvis hurried to greet them, looking flushed and out of breath. "Milord. A word."

She had been anticipating that once they were back where it was safe and warm, she and Noel could recapture their earlier romantic connection before the incident on the road. But that was dashed by Jarvis' pained expression. Something was terribly wrong.

Jarvis took Noel aside and, in hushed tones, discussed a surprise visitor Noel's father had had earlier in the evening.

She felt invisible and forgotten and confused.

Holly draped her coat over her arm, thinking that

all she wanted was a long soak in a warm bath and a good night's sleep. Tomorrow would be a new day.

She squared her shoulders as though braving a storm and approached Noel. "I apologize, but I'm tired. I'm going up to my room. I'll see you in the morning."

He just nodded.

She'd hoped he would ask her to wait for a while.

He didn't.

And that hurt.

She hesitated, but he'd already turned away to resume his conversation with Jarvis. She headed toward the stairs, taking one step in front of the other. This wasn't personal, she said to herself. But it felt personal. It felt like a rejection, and she didn't know why.

****

Noel watched Holly leave and head toward her room with a heavy heart. He knew he'd been abrupt. There was so much he wanted to say. On the trip back to the manor, they'd talked about the mystery of the tree and who might have cut it down. They'd danced around all sorts of possibilities, from an English-style Bigfoot to mischievous visiting Irish fairies. They avoided the obvious choice. Someone wanted to prevent Noel from reaching the manor, or at least delay him.

He'd thought that once they returned to the manor, they'd have a chance to settle in front of the fire and start again where they'd left off before the incident with the tree. Then when they returned to the manor everything went balls up.

He'd seen the mud on the boot scraper at the entrance to the manor. A little thing, until Jarvis told him of his father's unexpected visitor, Reginald Taylor.

Noel didn't believe in coincidences, and he didn't believe that Reggie had been here for a social visit. When Jarvis told Noel that his father wanted to talk to him as soon as he returned, Noel knew something was wrong.

He entered the library with a sense of foreboding. His father sat alone in front of the fire, staring at the flames and holding a snifter of amber-colored brandy. His father hated the taste of brandy.

"Hello, Father."

His father raised his head, turning it to the side slowly. "Did you have a fun sleigh ride back from town? Your mother loved them." His father's question seemed rhetorical. "Would you like a brandy?"

Noel declined the offer, debating whether he should share the odd occurrence concerning the tree that had been cut down deliberately. Then Noel glimpsed a document on the sofa beside his father, a document with Reginald Taylor's letterhead.

His unease increased. What was Reggie up to? "Jarvis said Reggie was here. What did he want?"

"You're direct. You're like your mother and grandfather in that regard." His father swirled the brandy in his glass. "I'm glad you're spending time with Holly. She is a nice woman. I haven't seen you this happy in a long time, and that got me thinking. Mistletoe Manor is a greedy mistress. She takes and takes, leaving little room for anything or anyone else. You deserve to be free of her. We both do."

Noel sat down on the sofa with Reggie's document between his father and himself. His father was in a strange mood tonight. His father had it wrong about the manor, though. She earned her own way. The problem was that his father gambled away more money than the estate could handle. Noel wanted to bring up that point but held back. His father was trying to change.

"We will turn the manor around," Noel said.

His father took a drink. "I disagree. I'm not blind. You spend all your time taking care of this place, neglecting your writing. With Holly, you have a real chance for a good life if you let go of this albatross."

Noel had difficulty taking a deep breath. Where was his father going with this line of thinking? "Mistletoe Manor is not an albatross. It is our home."

"It may be your home, but it was never mine," his father said, his voice rising. "I was an important man when I married your mother. I was a member of the House of Lords and was forced to take a leave from it in order to care for the manor."

Noel clenched his fists at his side. He had heard this before but would not allow his father's comment to go unchallenged. "Are you actually blaming your losing your seat in the House on the manor? You were asked to take a leave to get your gambling under control."

His father swirled the amber liquid in his glass again until it caught the firelight and shone like liquid gold. "You are right. I apologize. Old habits are difficult to break. Two steps forward and one back, as they say. I live with regrets. My biggest regret is not telling your mother how much I failed her and how much I loved her."

"Father…"

His father set the snifter on the table half finished. "No, I know what I've done. There was a time when your mother and I were happy. Sometimes I think too much was expected of me. I was supposed to accomplish great things when I married into the powerful Montgomery family. My parents were convinced I'd be Prime Minister one day. How could I tell them that the reason I married your mother was that I loved her and wanted nothing more than to manage the estate? But I always felt as though Mistletoe Manor was never really mine. After I lost my seat in the House, your grandfather saw to it that you would inherit the estate. For a long time, I resented him for it. Now, I'm grateful."

Noel had never seen his father so vulnerable. This was not an excuse for his gambling, but it showed the spiral that his father's life had taken. "Father, that is all in the past. With the infusion of cash from the Hemingway ornaments and the auction, we will be able to save the manor."

"The auction will no longer be necessary." His father handed Noel Reggie's document.

"Reginald suggested a safer, less risky proposition that will be better for both of us."

The walls of the library closed in around Noel. "Father, what have you done?"

"Reginald Taylor guaranteed we'd receive a fair price. Developers have wanted to buy portions of our estate even before your grandfather's time. Reginald has a buyer who will pay us cash for a section that runs along the river."

Noel felt as though someone had kicked him in the chest. He knew very well that his estate was prime for developers. He turned everyone down. "By the conditions of Grandfather's will, I control the land, and our home is not for sale."

"I told Reginald you'd say that, but you won't have

a choice. Since you were turned down by the bank, the auction was your only chance of raising money to pay off the loan. The manor and the lands might have been given to you, but with a few exceptions, the art and collectables—including the Hemingway ornaments—were gifts your mother gave to me. They won't be included in the auction without my approval. Son, this is for the best. I know you might not believe this, but I'm doing this for you. You will be out from under this albatross once and for all. You will have more time to devote to your writing, and I can rebuild my life, free from the constant reminder of my failings."

"Selling the lands Reggie proposes will doom the estate."

His father reached for his brandy. "True. There is another option. You can sign over the estate to Lady Catherine and walk away."

Chapter Forty-Three

The next morning, from the vantage point of his bedroom, Noel watched the sun struggle to rise over the horizon as though dreading the new day. He felt the same way. His father had effectively made it nearly impossible for the auction to succeed in raising the massive amount of money needed to pay off the loan. Noel didn't doubt that his father felt he was doing the right thing. He viewed the estate as an albatross that would ruin Noel's life as it had his.

On some level his father was right. Without the means to pay workers, operating the estate consumed more and more of Noel's time, with little time left to write. He'd tried to carve out space while Holly was here, so they could finish the novel, but he knew when spring came, the needs of the estate would demand all his attention.

He turned from the window to confront his computer. When he couldn't sleep, he'd taken another stab at the last chapter of the novel he and Holly were writing together and written two versions. With the idea in mind that with the sale of the estate he and Holly would continue their collaboration, he'd written a revision reflecting Holly's suggestions that more romance was needed. Instead of ending the chapter in a fiery car chase, the scene took place at a mountain wedding chapel.

Noel hadn't gone completely mushy, knowing his readers might gag, so instead of the bride wearing a fancy long wedding dress and veil, and the groom a black tux, they wore ski clothes. The chapter ended with the couple saying their vows.

Then along about three in the morning his thoughts had taken a darker turn as reality settled in the pit of his stomach. How could he give up his home without a fight? He'd told his father he had never considered the estate a burden, and he knew himself well enough to know that if he didn't at least try to save it, he'd turn into a hollow shell of a man. The auction was a great idea, but even that had been a long shot. Without the Hemingway ornaments and the more valuable artwork, the odds of success were not in his favor.

What the estate did have was land, and lots of it. He'd resisted selling off parcels to land developers, but these were desperate times. If he was selective, and only sold the lands on the outer edges of the estate, he might be able to retain the heart of the estate without jeopardizing its soul. Even with the sale, there would be rough times ahead, and he didn't want to drag Holly into that world.

When he'd come up with the idea of selling off land, he'd also written a second version of their last chapter.

Holly would like the beginning of the scene. She'd hate the ending. As soon as the couple said their I do's, there was a roar of an avalanche. It rolled down the mountain and crushed the wedding chapel and killed everyone inside.

He should consult Holly before sending his version to his editor. That would be the right thing to do with a coauthor. But he wanted her mad at him. So mad that the thought of collaborating on another novel, let alone wanting to continue their relationship, would be out of the question.

Noel straightened and rolled his head to ease the tension in his shoulders. He then entered his editor's email address, attached the chapter where the couple died in an avalanche, and pressed send. The next step was to tell everyone that they had to cancel the auction.

He stared out the window as the sun's rays moved over the frozen ground. No, the next step was to tell Holly. He should tell her first. He shook his head and turned his back to the window. He couldn't. He knew what she might say, and that would make it worse.

Chapter Forty-Four

Holly yawned and stretched, smiling as she descended the staircase to the main floor. She couldn't keep from smiling. Even the detour last night and the mystery of who cut down the tree couldn't dampen her mood. There had been that moment when they arrived at the manor and Noel hadn't said goodnight, but she was sure there was a logical explanation. The mystery of who had used a chainsaw to chop down the tree for one, and his father's surprise visitor for another. There was no doubt a logical explanation for both, she repeated in an attempt to shake the dark foreboding. She had every reason to feel positive.

She yawned again and felt as though she and Noel had taken their relationship to a new level, and it felt wonderful. They'd shared stories of their childhood, and Holly had a new understanding of how hard it must have been for Noel when he'd lost his mother so young. Surprisingly, Noel didn't blame his father for never being around, saying only that it was hard for both of them when his mother died. She'd loved him even more when he made that statement.

And then they'd made love.

A warm glow surged through her until she was certain that the color in her face matched the red piping on her Christmas sweater.

Did she love Noel?

She reached the bottom step and kept the answer at bay as though to examine it later. It was an important question and not to be taken lightly, but the signs were there. She felt as though she could talk to Noel about anything without judgment, and after their conversation last night, she suspected he felt the same way about her.

Enveloped in the Christmas spirit, she'd worn the Rudolf sweater her mother had brought with her as a gift for Holly. The tiny gold bells along the hem of the sweater chimed as Holly turned the corner and headed toward the sound of recorded Christmas music and laughter coming from the direction of the ballroom. Noel had suggested that it was the perfect location for the auction, with its open mirrored walls, high ceilings, and silver chandeliers.

Standing on the threshold of the ballroom, she gasped at its transformation. Her mother had been busy. The room no longer had that cold and formal feel so prevalent in some of the English homes.

Mistletoe hung from red ribbon beneath doorways and chandeliers, the fireplace mantel was draped with fir and pine boughs, and tables were covered with gold and green velvet. Holly even caught the smell of fresh baked sugar cookies on a side table with fresh brewed coffee.

The focal point was the tree in the center of the room, the tree she and Noel had cut down. Every available limb on the tree was covered with multicolored ornaments and lights made to resemble candles. The ornaments were shaped like miniature toy drums, brass horns, and toy soldiers, as well as handblown glass snowflakes and icicles. The tree resembled a photo Mable had shown Holly and her mother of the one Queen Victoria and Prince Albert had at Windsor Castle on Christmas Eve in eighteen hundred forty-eight. Everywhere Holly looked she noticed her mother's warm touch. Holly was so grateful her mother was here.

"There you are," her mother said, peeking out from around the tree. She set an ornament down on a cloud of tissue and motioned for Holly to join her. "How do you like the decorations?"

"Mom, you've created a winter wonderland. I wish you'd asked me for help."

Her mother shook her head. "Nonsense. You and Noel are busy with your novel. Besides, I've had plenty of help." She nodded toward a corner of the room where Simon and Catherine were bent together unpacking ornaments. "Those two were more than happy for the excuse to spend time together. They've been inseparable. Come. I want to show you some of the collectables I've chosen for the auction." She knelt and selected a vase from an opened box and handed it to Holly. "This little rosebud vase is so sweet. I think I'll bid on it myself."

Holly held it, examining it closer and smiled. "I can see why you like it so much. It's painted with pansies, your favorite flower."

"There's not going to be an auction," Noel's voice boomed over the music like thunder. He stood in the entry of the ballroom, his expression as frozen as the air outside the manor.

As soon as he'd made his game-changing announcement, he turned and stormed away.

The vase slipped from Holly's hand and shattered on the wood floor. In a daze, she knelt to pick up the broken pieces. No auction meant Noel would most likely lose the estate. What had happened between last night and this morning? And why, after everything that had happened between them, had he not told her? It was like he was shutting her out. Her heart felt like the pieces of ceramic vase shattered on the ground.

Her mother knelt beside Holly to help. "What is Noel talking about?"

Holly shook her head slowly as she gathered the pieces in her hand. Noel seemed changed since last night. He was like a stranger and hadn't acknowledged her presence. The haze lifted. What was going on?

Catherine brought a wicker wastebasket and had sent Simon for a broom. "I don't understand what could have changed Noel's mind about the auction."

"Me either," Holly said, dumping the shards of the vase into the wastebasket. "But I intend to find out."

Holly left the ballroom and raced after Noel, having a pretty good idea where he'd gone. When they weren't writing, he spent his free time taking care of the horses and repairing the manor and its grounds. He never complained, and what was clear after their conversations last night was how much he loved Mistletoe Manor. Keeping it running was back-breaking work, but for Noel it was a labor of love, and that's why canceling the auction didn't make sense.

On a dead run, she entered the kitchen and stopped short. As she suspected, he was in the kitchen filling a thermos with coffee.

"Why are you cancelling the auction?" she demanded.

He screwed on the thermos lid and headed for the back door. "Not now."

She rushed to intercept him and block his exit. "Last night you thought the auction was a good idea."

"Last night the world hadn't come to an end."

She stood her ground and crossed her arms over her chest. He was being overly dramatic, which was unlike him. There were dark circles under his eyes as though he hadn't slept. He said the world had come to an end, and it looked like the world had also crushed him under its heel.

"Noel. Please talk to me."

He hesitated, then looked even more tired than before as his shoulders drooped. "You deserve to know. I should not have gotten you and your family involved. The auction was a dream from the start and was bound to unravel. I should have been suspicious at the meeting with Catherine yesterday when Reggie suggested I deed over the lands on the west side of the property. I was left the land, livestock, and physical dwellings, while my father owns the contents of the manor, right down to the silverware and antique chamber pots. Reggie paid my father a visit last night while we were making a detour around the tree in the road. He convinced my father that an auction was a bad idea. Long story made short: we can't have an auction when we don't have anything to sell." Noel reached for the doorknob.

Holly put her hand over his to keep him from turning the knob. No wonder Noel was so concerned last night when he was talking with Jarvis. Noel didn't trust Reggie, and it sounded like he had good reason. The timing of Reggie's appearance was suspicious, to say the least. It couldn't be a coincidence that she and Noel were forced to take a detour, delaying their arrival, while Reggie was paying Noel's father a visit.

But the question she was about to ask Noel seemed too farfetched.

She lowered her voice. "Do you think Reggie is the one who cut down the tree so he would have time to talk to your father before you got here?"

Noel scrubbed his face with both hands as though to wake himself from a bad dream. "Probably. It's something that wanker would do. He couldn't have done it alone, though. I've reached out to my friends in town to see if they've heard anything."

"We could talk to your father—convince him to change his mind..."

Noel moved Holly away from the door gently. "You always are the optimistic one. Promise me you'll never lose that quality. We might convince my father to change his mind, but even if we did, there's no guarantee the auction would generate the money we need. On that point my father was right." He opened the door. "I have to check the horses."

She followed him outside and paused as he walked away. "What will you do?"

"The only thing that is left. Sell some of the land."

She pressed her hand to her mouth to quiet a sob. She felt the pain in his voice and heard the deep-throated sound of defeat as Noel let loose a string of British swear words.

Chapter Forty-Five

Pacing over the rug in her bedroom wasn't working. Midafternoon and Holly wasn't any closer to a decision regarding the ending for *Love Is Lost*. She'd given up trying to consult Noel. She hadn't spoken to him again since he'd disappeared last night to talk with his father again. When she'd tried to find Noel this morning, Jarvis, being the perfect gatekeeper, had told her Noel was busy with the estate.

She paused at the bookshelf where she'd placed *Whispers on a Pillow*. Readers always asked her what she considered the least favorite part of writing a novel. That was a tough question. She loved almost every part and for different reasons, from the sunny-faced newness of creating characters as they explored their world to the overcoming of obstacles thrown in their path. She even loved the editing part when the story was complete and it was time to expand the characters' emotions and layer the story with world-building textures.

If there was a part that was not a favorite, however, it was the scenes near the end where the characters believed they'd fail. Those scenes were gut-wrenching. When she put her characters through the ordeal of failure, it felt as though she were going through it with them.

Were she and Noel going through a similar dark

moment? Was that why his avoiding her was hitting her so hard?

She needed a distraction to pull her out of her doldrums. Holly faced the bookshelf. And speaking of avoiding, she'd avoided reading the last entries in Madelyn's journal, thinking that there wouldn't be a happy ending. But maybe she was wrong.

She reached for the journal and settled on the window seat, opening to the last section. Madelyn and Willingsworth were in their favorite rendezvous area by a mountain stream. Madelyn had brought a basket of food, and Willingsworth had laid a blanket over the ground.

A warm summer sun filtered through the willow trees and glittered over the pond like crystals hung from a chandelier.

Madelyn snatched her clothes to her bare chest. "You can't leave me."

Willingsworth knelt beside her. "We've talked this over. I want you to come with me. I've booked us passage…"

Her eyes brimmed with tears. "I thought after today…" Her heart was breaking. He asked the impossible. "I'll tell my father that we love each other. That we want to marry."

"Your father would never approve your marrying someone from the working class."

"We'll run away to Gretna Green in Scotland and marry. When we're married, and if I'm with child, he'll have to take us in."

"I'll not rely on another man's charity. More likely your father will cast you out. Come with me. We can make a new life for ourselves in America."

Tears fell down her checks and she let them fall. How could she make him understand? "Without my father's support, we'll be poor. You can't ask that of me."

The scene ended with those words.

Holly fingered the water smudges on the page that looked like they may have been from long-ago tears. Her own eyes brimmed over. What was she going to do?

Chapter Forty-Six

She'd done the unthinkable.

The last few days had been difficult. Holly had replaced *Whispers on a Pillow* on the bookshelf, vowing to eradicate the story of Madelyn and Willingsworth from her thoughts. She sat in her room looking out over the dreary gray winter's day. Snow had turned to rain, and the English gardens gave the impression of a stately noblewoman dressed formally to accept mourners for the lord of the manor's funeral. The image fit how she felt. Last night, in a puddle of tears, she'd sent her editor the last chapter of the novel without telling Noel.

Since Noel's announcement, everyone was avoiding each other and had confined themselves to minimal association. Noel's father spent his time in his rooms. Her mother and stepfather spent most of their time in town, and Simon and Catherine were at her estate more often than elsewhere. Noel avoided Holly so successfully it was as though he'd become invisible. She understood it was painful for him to have to sell a portion of his lands, but what had that to do with their relationship?

Holly drummed her fingers on her desk beside her laptop, re-reading the email reminder from Mable. Today she and Noel were meeting in town for a book-signing event, and she knew Noel would not disappoint

Mable—at least Holly hoped not. This would be Holly's chance to find out why Noel was avoiding her.

She glanced at the clock on the wall. The book signing wasn't scheduled for several hours, but Mable wanted her authors at her store within the hour for photographs and an interview with the local arts and entertainment reporter. Usually she looked forward to these events. Not today.

This was the first time she was participating in a book signing with Noel, and she'd been up since dawn trying on different outfits. She'd settled on a strapless dress that was more appropriate for a dinner date at a fancy restaurant than a book signing. It was low cut and Christmas red. She considered a different dress and then changed her mind.

Red was a color that oozed confidence, and she was not going to feel guilty about sending her chapter to her editor without telling Noel.

A flock of birds lifted into the sky, and Holly turned toward the sound. Noel and his father had entered the garden and strolled in the direction of a three-tiered water fountain that had been turned off for the winter.

Unbearably handsome, Noel stood at the bottom of the steps near the door, dressed in pressed jeans and a navy-blue sports jacket and tie. His expression was unreadable and looked chiseled from granite. His father wore a wool overcoat and was more animated. Occasionally, he swiped at his face as though he'd been crying.

From conversations she'd pieced together from her mother, her stepfather, and Jarvis, she'd expanded on what Noel had said the day he'd announced the auction was cancelled. Noel's father felt he was doing the right thing by preventing them from having the auction. But he'd underestimated Noel's determination to keep the majority of the estate. Simon told her that Noel's friends in town had discovered that Reggie had been responsible for cutting the tree down. And when Catherine found out the part Reginald Taylor and his associate had played, she'd fired him and reported their conduct to the authorities.

Father and son moved behind a glass-domed greenhouse and out of Holly's line of sight.

The real tragedy, in Holly's mind, was the fractured relationship between Noel and his father.

She turned back to her laptop to check messages one more time. She hadn't heard from Noel, and since he was occupied with his father, she doubted they'd be driving into town together. Jarvis might be able to drive her, and if not, she'd take a taxi.

A joint email message from her editor and Noel's appeared on the screen.

She took a steady breath, bracing for her editor's comments. No matter how many books she'd written, she was always nervous about her editor's response. Concerned about meeting their deadline and unable to consult Noel, she'd sent in her version of the last chapter last night. Or at least that's the reason she gave herself. She knew the real reason was that she was angry and hurt and striking out.

She mentally held her breath.

In the email, their editors praised Holly and Noel's storytelling skills, the development of their characters, the suspenseful plotlines, and the exciting twists and turns. It wasn't that their editors hadn't praised them in the past, it was that the email seemed to be building to a big, fat "but."

And then she saw something unexpected in the next to the last paragraph. According to Noel's editor, Noel had emailed his version yesterday as well.

"How dare he!" Holly shouted.

You didn't tell him either, an annoying voice in her head offered in a snarky tone.

"How could I tell him?" Her voice rose an octave higher. "He wouldn't talk to me. I had to turn in something."

She counted to ten to get her pulse rate under control and turned toward her bedroom door, half expecting Jarvis or Clara to burst in and ask why she was shouting. She'd have to explain that she was not losing her mind: she was an author.

She ignored the prick of guilt and rising panic and scrolled down to the last paragraph. Their comments were short and to the point. Their editors loved the first two-thirds of the book. They hated both Holly's and Noel's version of the last third, especially the last chapter. They'd used the word "hated," and for added emphasis had both underlined and bolded the word.

She sank against her chair, glancing outside. Noel and his father were nowhere in sight. What were she and Noel going to do now? Neither one of them could afford to return the advance.

Changing their names and disappearing to a remote corner of the world only happened in movies or books, or to people who were as rich as kings, queens, or owners of tech companies. She sent a short email reminder to Noel about the book signing, adding that if he couldn't make it, they still needed to talk today. She called Noel's cell, and when it went to voicemail, she left a message and a text message as well. She hadn't gone into any details other than that it was urgent.

Holly closed her laptop and put it in her messenger-style briefcase, reached for her coat, and left her bedroom. She searched for what she would say to Noel as she headed down the hallway toward the staircase. The book signing would be neutral territory. Had Noel received the same email she had? She'd forgotten to check if he'd been copied by their editors. If he hadn't, she could explain why she'd sent her version without telling him.

Would he be as upset as she had been at first?

She buttoned her coat and slung her briefcase across her shoulder as she hurried down the stairs. She knew a big part of her had been upset that Noel had sent in a chapter without telling her. Trust was broken. And since they'd both broken that trust, they were even. Would Noel see it that way? Regardless, they had to turn in another version by midnight tonight or lose their advance.

No pressure.

She reached the bottom step just as Noel appeared. Her heart leapt to her throat. What was she going to say to him? His expression remained unreadable except for a spark of a smile in his eyes when his gaze met hers. Or was this her imagination playing tricks, more wishful thinking on her part?

"Did you read the email from our editors?" she said as she approached him.

He held the door open for her. "We should go. Mable insists that her authors be on time."

Chapter Forty-Seven

Mable opened the door to her authors, who swept through the entrance as though fueled by angry winds. Their emotions electrified the air. Disappointment, hurt, and anger seeped out of every pore. And there was love. Mable could see it when they glanced at each other when they thought the other person wasn't looking. Something had happened, and they didn't know how to make it right.

The first time she'd seen the couple had been the day Holly arrived in Derby. Mable had noticed how they'd looked at each other then. In fact, everyone in the bookstore that day had noticed, and the town was abuzz with the rumor that, for the first time, Noel was falling in love. It was not the attraction of two people meeting for the first time. Rather, it was that ah-ha moment when hearts realized they'd met their soulmates.

Then Mable had seen them again in town the afternoon Noel had taken Holly for a sleigh ride. They looked at each other in that happily-ever-after way that made people smile just watching the two of them together.

But something had happened between then and now.

Mable didn't know what had occurred, but the mother hen side of her vowed to get to the bottom of it.

Young people could be so silly sometimes. Love, even the possibility of love, should never be taken for granted.

She'd arranged the tables side by side and included the most recent titles of Noel's and Holly's books. She had made a large, poster-size cover of the book they were writing together, scheduled for release in the fall of next year. It was a Christmas-themed cover in greens and reds, with a couple kissing under a sprig of mistletoe. Very romantic. Very hopeful.

The poster was the first casualty.

Noel carried it and the easel to a corner, turning the cover to face the wall. Next, he moved the table with his books to the far side of the room. Not to be outdone, Holly gathered the bookmarks imprinted with their new book cover and tossed them into the wastebasket.

Mable had seen better behavior from children. She'd known Noel since he had been in nappies, and although she'd met Holly only recently, she'd followed her career since its beginning. Noel and Holly were good people, and it was clear they were hurting.

Mable had to make this right. She held up her hands. "What is going on with you two?"

Silence frosted the air as Holly and Noel stared at each other from across the room. And as though a dam had burst, they both started talking at the same time.

Holly pointed to Noel. "He emailed his ending chapter to his editor without telling me."

"What about you? You did the same thing without giving me a word of warning."

Holly put her hands on her hips. "I'll give you a word. Several, in fact. I told you that my version is the best for a romance ending."

A muscle tightened along Noel's jawline. "My readers will revolt and never read another one of my books without an action-style cliff-hanger. My characters kiss and marry. That's romantic."

Holly held a pen in her hand so tightly Mable thought it might snap in half.

"I read your chapter," Holly said with deadly calm. "My editor was kind enough to include it in her email. After your characters were married, they died in an avalanche. And for the record, my readers will also revolt if I crush my characters under a mountain of snow. Your readers will forgive you. They'll see the kiss as a one-time thing. A blip. You will write more novels where you are free to blow up your characters into tiny pieces instead of having them develop lasting relationships. All will be right in your world. I won't be that lucky. My career will be as exciting as a steady diet of cold toast, runny eggs, and fried tomatoes."

"Ignoring your slam on a traditional English breakfast, even if that were true, your career won't be over simply because you aren't writing romance. You're a great writer," he continued in a louder voice. "You can write in another genre."

"You don't get it," she said, her voice rising to match Noel's. "I like writing romance. I like the journey of helping my characters find their happily-ever-after."

It was worse than Mable thought. She stepped between the warring authors. "Please keep your voices down. My customers will be arriving soon. You mentioned that you sent your scenes to your editors. What did they say? Which one did they like best?"

Holly stomped over to her table and slouched down

behind her books, using them as a shield. Noel did the same, only he stared at his books with such intensity that Mable thought the books might burst into flames.

Mable slowly nodded, assessing the authors. "Your editors hated both endings."

Holly and Noel's gazes locked on Mable. The panic in their eyes was as clear as day.

Holly sat up straighter and fingered the pages on one of her books. "My editor hated the romance ending. She said the characters were hiding their feelings from each other."

"My editor said the same thing," Noel said, his voice barely audible. "She added that she didn't think anyone would mind that I killed off my characters."

Mable kept her voice as neutral as she could manage as her suspicions grew. "How do you feel about your editors' comments?"

He heaved a sigh. "My editor said I took too much time describing the avalanche and the condition of the bodies."

Holly set her pen aside. "My editor said the romance felt forced."

"What if you combine the scenes? Your editors wanted you to write the story together, so write it together. Maybe you'll discover more about your characters and how they feel about one another." To Holly and Noel's credit, they didn't seem to object to her suggestion. "When do you have to turn in your finished chapter?"

"Midnight tonight," Noel and Holly said at the same time.

"There has to be kissing," Holly added, sitting up straighter.

"They can kiss before they are buried in snow."

Holly rolled her eyes, and Mable fought against doing the same.

"Absolutely not," Holly said, throwing a book in his direction. It collided with his stack of books, toppling them like a wrecking ball.

"Hey," Noel said, springing to his feet and out of the way of books toppling to the floor. "Death and mayhem provide a dramatic ending."

"And will ensure that there isn't a sequel because you've killed everyone off." Holly paused, then stood abruptly, knocking a few of her own books over. "That's it, isn't it? You don't want our novel to have a sequel. More to the point, you don't want us to work together anymore."

"Holly," Noel began, "you know the situation. I plan sell land to repay the loan to Catherine's husband's estate. But my father and I are not out of the woods. We have been working out the ongoing operational expenses and developing sources of income but agree that the next few years will be challenging. I won't have time to write. It's better this way if we end our story without the possibility of a sequel."

Holly had been arranging books on her table as though only half-listening. But when Noel finished, she looked over at him and her expression had softened. "You mentioned your father. Have the two of you made peace?"

Noel loosened his tie as though it were too tight. "We've made a start and are focusing on a path forward. I'm not sure how it will look, but we're trying. We also talked about plans for the estate, from horse breeding to opening a boutique hotel. Everything is on the table, including my mother's vintage clothing museum." Noel removed his tie and tossed it over a pile of books. "But it will take money and time."

"What about us?"

"Didn't you hear the part where I said we can't work together anymore?"

Silence descended over the room as Noel and Holly avoided eye contact.

Mable looked first at Noel and then at Holly. Her earlier suspicions took a turn. The idiot boy was deliberately trying to make a mess of things. He was blowing up his relationship with Holly before it had a chance to grow.

Noel's parents once had considered breaking up, until Mable heard the news and intervened. She'd known the courtship had suffered a rocky start and decided to help. She'd always had an instinct about these sorts of things. She knew when a couple was meant for each other.

She'd made up an excuse for Noel's parents to pick her up, and then had made sure the auto they drove broke down after they dropped her off. It helped that it was raining, and they had to find shelter in an abandoned cottage. The abandoned cottage just happened to be stocked with wood for the fire and had food in the cupboards.

If her intervention had worked once, it might work again.

Mable interrupted the silence. "It is time for the two of you to take a break. People won't be arriving for your book signing for at least two more hours, and I'll reschedule the arts and entertainment interview for after the book signing. I suggest the two of you go into my private kitchen and fix yourselves a lovely cup of tea. I like my authors at least behaving cordially to one another when they meet their readers."

She interpreted their lack of objection as a good sign.

Mable walked them upstairs to her living quarters. The authors were giving each other the silent treatment, while Mable explained that her kitchen would be a quiet place to relax. She added that she'd take care of delaying anyone arriving early for the book signing.

She left them in the kitchen, making a mental note that if this didn't work out, she'd phone her mechanic friend and the owner of the cottage.

Chapter Forty-Eight

Mable's kitchen was as cozy as the bookstore and reminded Holly of her mother's back home. There was a window over the sink where geraniums were wintering in pots along the sill. A small wood table stood in the center of the room with two matching chairs and a lace tablecloth. In the corner, Mable's white cat, Shakespeare, lay curled on a rug fast asleep. On any other day, Holly would have been thrilled to spend time here. Today, however, the well-loved kitchen made her want to cry.

Noel held his laptop under his arm as Holly took hers out of her messenger bag and set it on the table, rewinding their conversation. Noel didn't want to work with her after they finished this book. The news hit her harder than she would have expected. It felt like she was losing not just her best friend but someone with whom she had envisioned building a life together.

Noel set his laptop on the table. "I'll make tea." The distance in his voice seemed to pull the air from the room.

Holly nodded and traced her fingers over her laptop, resisting the impulse to throw it out the window or at Noel's head. She didn't care if she and Noel never wrote another word together. She cared about him. Why couldn't he see that? He had that British stiff upper lip attitude, and it was getting on her last nerve. Well, two could play at that game.

She lifted her chin and drained her voice of emotion. "Mable mentioned that she'd made scones with clotted cream for us, and to help ourselves."

Noel nodded in response, filled up the teakettle and set it on the stove to heat, and then reached for the tin of loose-leaf black tea.

They were as formal as two strangers. She preferred their arguing. At least then she still felt like they were together. At least then they had a chance to realize they belonged together.

Who was she kidding?

The infuriating man had closed the door on their relationship. She uncovered the fresh baked scones and placed them on the table beside a jar of raspberry jam. The scones reminded her of the ones her mother had made for her before Holly left for England. That seemed a lifetime ago.

She opened the refrigerator and took out a large bowl of clotted cream that looked like it had been made from scratch. Because it was hard to buy in the U.S., Holly had planned to make it herself after she and her mother visited the Empress Hotel in Victoria, B.C. for high tea. She'd gone so far as to purchase the ingredients, but when she learned it would take three days to produce one cup, she changed her mind. She closed the refrigerator door and retraced her steps to the table.

She was behaving as mechanically as Noel but didn't know what else to do. If she were writing a scene where her characters were in this predicament, she'd create a third element to force them to deal with their issues. Maybe Noel's exploding car and building plotlines weren't such a bad idea.

"Would you mind setting the table?" he said.

She glared at Noel's back. "Delighted," she said through gritted teeth. She set the clotted cream next to the scones and stomped over to the cupboard, yanked open the door, and took out plates, cups, and a matching teapot. Juggling them in her arms, she slammed the door, rattling the plates.

She winced, feeling a smidge guilty about losing her temper as she set everything on the table. She wouldn't forgive herself if she broke one of Mable's plates. The china had a red-rose pattern faded with age as though it had been in Mable's family for generations. Imagining generations had sat at this table drinking tea, solving problems, and sharing their dreams calmed her a little. It also made her weepy.

She swiped at her tears and set the table while Noel poured warm water from the faucet into the teapot and set it aside. They were behaving politely around each other now, and she hated it. She pressed her hand against her heart. Why did the thought of never seeing or hearing from Noel again hurt so much?

Because you love him, came the voice in her head. But instead of the voice sounding accusatory as it had this morning, it was gentle and sad. She cleared her throat, searching for a neutral topic and settled on the lovers from *Whispers on a Pillow*.

"Mable had more news on Madelyn and Willingsworth. Despite the last entry I read, I wanted to believe that Madelyn and Willingsworth found a way to be together and live happily ever after and asked Mable if she could keep searching."

"What happened in the last entry?" he said,

bringing the brewed tea over to the table and pouring tea into first her cup and then his. "Any clues?"

Holly waited until she'd taken a sip of the fortifying tea. "Willingsworth asked Madelyn to come with him to the Americas, and she refused. But I'm not giving up on them. A bit of good news. Mable found a ship's manifest with an entry listing Willingsworth. It looked like he was traveling alone. However, there was a curious entry farther down the page that we almost missed. The entry said simply: M. Willingsworth, as though the person didn't want authorities to know that she was a woman. My next step is to check on records for Ellis Island."

Noel settled down opposite Holly at the table. "Everyone should have someone like you in their life. You never give up on love. Through your lens, I'm beginning to understand that love is always tested, and those who don't run from it but embrace it find their soulmate."

Tears brimmed in her eyes and traveled down her cheek. She'd found her soulmate only to lose him.

"You're crying. What's wrong?"

She shrugged it away. "Nothing," she mumbled. But there was something wrong, and if he had half a brain, he'd know it too. She was falling apart. Her eyes blurred as she reached for a scone, then shook her head. She gripped the side of the table. "No, I'm not okay. You're giving up on us," she said, gaining momentum. "You're using the book we're writing together and financial concerns as an excuse, and I won't let you. You're afraid. Well, so am I. Relationships are scary. Class traditions and parental authority conspired to keep Madelyn and Willingsworth apart, but I want to believe that they found a way to be together. Love finds a way."

He wiped his hands on a towel and inched toward her, forming his words carefully. "I've explained the situation…"

"You have explained nothing," she snapped back. She refused to dance around the issue any longer. "You're having financial issues. Well, welcome to the real world."

He folded his arms across his chest as he peered at her. "That is typical. You think because I live in a large house that I've never experienced hardship or worried how to pay property taxes, mortgages, put food on the table, let alone pay Jarvis and Clara's salaries. I can't rely on the money I make as an author. It's only as good as my next hit. Right now, I'm selling books, but how long will it last? I need something more stable. If I can turn the estate into a working farm and breed horses, the manor would not only survive, it would thrive. But that's a big if, and I can't ask you to take that chance."

Not one word of what he said deterred her. On the contrary, she loved him more for his determination to save his home and protect those he cared about. But he was an idiot. "Couples face problems together. That's what couples do when they love each other. You say you won't have time to write, and I get it. You have a lot of work ahead, turning the estate around. Take a break from writing. The great thing being an author is that we're not like professional athletes who have a small window of time when they will be at their peak performance. We're authors. We get better with age."

She paused for breath as a plan took shape that hopefully would pull him out of his doldrums and back into her arms. She leaned toward him with a new sense of purpose. "But right now, we have an immediate problem. We have a deadline, and according to our editors, the entire last chapter has to be rewritten. Our editors complained that although our characters said they loved each other, the emotion wasn't there when they kissed. We have to find a way for our characters to connect." She let the words linger in the air, hoping he'd come to the same conclusion she had.

He opened his laptop to his last chapter. "We could have them kiss right after they say they love each other."

She pressed her lips together to keep the smile at bay. Pleased she'd gotten through, she opened her laptop. "Look at you. That's the perfect place for a kiss. That still doesn't address the emotion. We have to find a way to tap into how they are feeling."

"We could describe the explosion-type sound of an avalanche as it descends the mountain slopes and connect it to how they are feeling. The idea of being buried alive would certainly get my heart pumping with emotion."

"Me too," she nodded slowly.

He looked so serious she almost laughed. It was obvious they had been working out emotional issues and how they felt about each other through their characters. It was no wonder their editors felt that the characters in *Love is Lost* were struggling. The authors were also struggling.

She dared a glance in Noel's direction. He scrolled through the scene on his computer, adding a word or deleting a phrase. He was all business as he sipped tea or took a bite out of a scone. It was time for the next step.

"How about we pretend that we are our characters and practice their kiss?" Holly said. "We can use your idea and pretend our characters are aware an avalanche is headed their way."

His eyebrows shot up as he gulped down the last of his scone. "I beg your pardon?"

Her suggestion had taken him by surprise. If the rise in color on his face was any indication, he was thinking that the last time they kissed, they couldn't stop. Perfect. She plunged forward, keeping her voice professional, although all she could see in her mind's eye was how Noel looked naked.

"My editor said she couldn't feel the emotion when our characters kissed. Maybe if there was more emotion, our editors wouldn't mind if the characters died." She cringed at the thought of what she was about to say. "We could play up a *Romeo and Juliet* kind of ending."

He leaned back in his chair. "You made it clear that you hated *Romeo and Juliet*."

She still hated the tragic outcome of that stupid play, but that was a discussion for another day. "I'm willing to look at other options. Are you?"

Chapter Forty-Nine

Holly alternated between the need for patience and stripping naked.

Noel had spent the last hour tweaking a scene in the ending chapter and obsessing over comma placements. It was like working with a grammar-check robot. They'd drained one teapot and had put on the kettle to boil more water, avoiding Holly's suggestion that they pretend to be their characters and kiss in order to bring more emotion into the last scene of their last chapter.

She arrived at a solution between allowing Noel's preoccupation with editing to continue and jumping on the table and performing a striptease.

To get Noel's attention, she scraped her chair over the wood floor and when he looked up, she feigned an apology. While he was still focused on her, and with the pretense of getting more comfortable in her chair, she hiked her strapless red dress higher up her thighs until it was borderline indecent. For good measure she took a deep breath, knowing full well that her breasts would press against the dress's thin silk fabric and threaten to spill over.

Noel dropped his teacup on the saucer and fumbled to keep it from falling. Hot liquid sloshed and spilled over his hand. He swore under his breath, then stood, adjusted his jeans, and left the table.

She hid a smile as she lifted her teacup to her mouth and sipped as though she hadn't noticed the bulge in his jeans. Good. The man was human after all. There was hope.

With his back to her, he knelt to pet the white cat curled on the rug. Shakespeare lifted his chin to allow Noel to scratch behind one ear as Noel huffed out a sigh. "Holly, the last few days without you have been torture."

She choked on her tea. All this time she'd felt alone. Her cup rattled on the saucer as she set it in place. "I've missed you."

His nod was a single dip of his head as his focus remained on Shakespeare. "I've spent the time thinking about how we first connected. In your introductory email, you never once talked about yourself. You talked about your family and how amazing they were. You talked about your community and how important it was to be grateful for the blessings in life. I'd been having a rough day, and you were so positive. I couldn't believe someone like you existed in the world."

Holly was surprised by his admission, today of all days. Her heart warmed over his words. She hadn't any idea her email had meant so much to him. She remembered feeling nervous that day. She had been under deadline for another project, and her mother had made a batch of double fudge brownies. Building her courage to email her coauthor for the first time, she'd eaten half the batch.

She'd researched the reclusive bachelor and discovered he'd won countless writing awards and his books had routinely made the *USA Today* and *New York Times* lists. His email had arrived first, and it was so friendly, as though they'd known each other all their lives. He asked about her day, sharing that he'd helped give birth to a colt, and then joked that the life of an author was not as glamorous as readers envisioned. She'd developed a crush on him before his email ended.

She scooted to the edge of her chair. "I liked your emails, too. I felt like I could share things with you that I could never share with anyone else. My mother and stepfather said one of the reasons their relationship worked was because they were pen pals first. Before the internet, before emails and texting, people wrote to each other. They poured out their hearts on paper."

Her comments were met with silence. She clamped her mouth shut to prevent saying more, her pulse rising over the comparison she'd made between herself and Noel and her mother and stepfather. Had she said too much by using the comparison? Only time would tell. She didn't regret what she'd said. In fact, it proved her point. She had to make Noel understand that their relationship wasn't over. It was just beginning.

To give herself something to do, she spread clotted cream over a scone and took a fortifying bite. She licked her lips and met his gaze. He'd returned to the table as quietly as any cat. Annoying man. She washed down the remaining scone in her mouth with tea. "Back to business. Our editors expect our last chapter by midnight tonight. As agreed, we should practice our characters' kiss." She hesitated. "In the interest of trying to describe how our characters feel."

He looked as nervous as she felt, as though this were their first kiss.

Noel mumbled what sounded like an okay as he leaned in and kissed her tentatively, almost shyly. This kiss felt different. Was it because she feared it might be their last?

The kiss deepened.

Her senses jolted alive. She was back in the forest under the cover of stars. Awakened emotions sent memories of their night of passion racing through her until she couldn't catch her breath. Warmth swirled around the fringes as though waiting for more, threatening to ignite the very air she breathed.

His lips trailed over her cheek to whisper in her ear. "I should probably put my arms around you," he said, his voice husky with emotion.

Her skin, already sensitized under his touch, shivered in anticipation. "Good idea. I'll write that into the scene."

The realization that he wanted to end their relationship woke her from passion's haze. She didn't know when the friendship she felt for Noel had changed into something stronger. All she knew was that she loved him, and she wouldn't allow him to give up on them so easily.

She pulled back from his embrace, creating the distance she needed. "I can't lose you," she blurted. "I told you that I believe with all my heart that any financial difficulty you face, we can face together. Is there something else I'm missing? Does it have to do with our book? I shouldn't have sent in the last chapter without consulting you. That was awful. I was so angry and hurt and confused, but that is no excuse. I'm so sorry."

He reached out to take her hands. "Holly. You had every right to feel the way you did. I'm the one who needs to beg your forgiveness. I sent in my version because I knew it would drive you away."

The confirmation tore down her last walls. "I can't lose you," she repeated. "If you want to blow up our characters, bury them in a mountain of snow, ash, or lava, I'll figure out how to deal with my readers."

He blinked as though seeing her for the first time as he raked his hands through his hair. "You'd do that?"

"Absolutely!"

"I've been a daft fool, haven't I? I don't want to lose you either."

Steam poured from the kettle on the stove, and it whistled, the sound bringing a smile to her lips. She wanted to sing along with the kettle. "The daftest. Particularly, if daft is a British slang word that means a complete and utter fool."

His laugh rolled gently through the room as he stood and removed the kettle from the burner. "If it isn't, it should be."

Her heart thundered in her chest so loudly she was certain Mable could hear it downstairs in the bookstore. In every story she'd ever written the hero was the first to declare his love. That was the rule.

It was a stupid rule.

"I love you," she blurted before she lost her nerve. "And I know that you love me but are too stubborn or too proud or too *something* to admit it. We're going to work this out together, because I'm not leaving."

"Brilliant!" He moved toward her slowly. "Sweetheart, I love you too, and you continue to take me by surprise, and I'm loving every minute. And for the record, if you had left, I would have chased you to the ends of the earth."

She was in his arms, reeling from him calling her

his sweetheart and his declaration of love. "Noel...I..."

He kissed her with a smile on his lips. The kiss fast-tracked from light as air to urgent need in the span of a few breaths. She tasted the sweet promise of forever in the way his mouth moved against hers and then stilled, inching away as he held her gaze.

He leaned his forehead against hers, spreading his hand on the small of her back, pulling her against him. "Do you know my father called me a fool and a few other names I can't repeat, and he was right. It was the first thing we agreed on in a long time. That's when I knew."

She'd known for a long time.

He brushed a kiss over her lips and down the side of her neck to her bare shoulder, warming her skin and flaming her senses. She tilted her head to the side as shivers of delight chased over her skin. Was this really happening?

She couldn't stop smiling and didn't want to. It was as though she'd been dreaming of this moment all her life, and now it was here, all she could think about was the miracle that the man she loved actually loved her in return.

He lifted her onto his lap and kissed the base of her neck. "I should tell you that I'll want to take my time." He kissed her shoulder, his warm breath caressing her skin. Shivers of passion shimmered over her as he pulled her against him. She felt as though she'd known him all her life. Pressed against him, she slid her arm up his, feeling his muscles harden against her touch.

He was a man of his word and was taking his time. She raised her eyes to meet his fire-stoked gaze. There was heat in his expression that fanned the flames in her heart. "I love you with every breath I take," he said.

She let his words blossom like the unfolding rose petals under the tender touch of a summer sun. "You're not alone. We are in this together." She knew she had told him this before, but this time his eyes softened, and she knew he'd embraced them with his heart and soul.

"We are in this together," he said, repeating her words. "I want to make love to you."

She scooped a dollop of clotted cream from the bowl on the table with her finger and touched his nose, grinning. "About time."

He seemed taken back, his head cocked to the side, as he wiped the cream from his nose with the back of his hand. "I tell you I love you and want to make love to you, and you cover me with cream?"

"It is very good clotted cream. It tastes nutty and sweet." She paused. "Where are you going?"

He crossed over to the refrigerator, opened the door, and scanned the interior. "Ah, here it is." He shook a canister of whipping cream and then aimed it in her direction.

"What are you doing?" She scrambled to her feet and placed her chair between them as he took aim. She ducked but not in time. Foaming whipped cream landed on her bare shoulder.

His gaze was mischievous as he shoved the chair aside and strode toward her. The chair tilted and crashed to the floor, startling the cat. It meowed and scampered out of the kitchen toward the stairs as Holly reached for the bowl of clotted cream.

She held out the bowl as though it were a shield. "Noel. Let's talk about this. We have a book signing in an hour."

He shook the canister again. "I agree we don't have as much time as I'd like." He leaned over and licked the cream off her shoulder. "You taste good. I wonder how you'd taste covered in raspberry jam?"

She wondered what he would taste like covered in chocolate.

Holly didn't know if it was the way his tongue slowly licked away the cream covering her skin or the visual of her doing the same thing to him that awakened every nerve in her body and made her lean into his touch. Lips parted, she gripped the bowl of clotted cream in one hand and clung to him with the other.

Footsteps echoed on the wood stairs as the door to the kitchen flung open. "I was coming upstairs with your package when I heard something fall," Mable said, opening the door wider. "What's going on in…" Her voice froze. She stood on the threshold to the kitchen, with the cat at her feet. "Oh. Never mind." Her cheeks pinkened as she avoided making eye contact. She shoved the package into Noel's arms and closed the door.

"Mable," Noel shouted. "Can you delay the book signing?"

"Will do," came the swift reply, followed by footsteps descending the stairs.

Holly should feel embarrassed that Mable had walked in on them. She wasn't. She was glad. She wanted everyone to know that she and Noel were in love. "The package looks familiar."

He nodded slowly as he set the box on the counter. "It's the Hemingway ornament box." His voice was quiet as he read the note attached. He shook his head again. "My father is giving us the ornaments to sell.

Can you believe it?"

She rested her head on his back as she gave him a hug. She loved that he had used the word *us*. "Yes, I can. Your father loves you very much and only wants your happiness. I think he was confused before on how to make that happen."

Noel turned and took her in his arms. "You never doubted that my father loved me. I love that family is so important to you."

She reached up to kiss him. "And I love that you embraced my family as though they were your own. You have a good heart, Mr. Atteberry. Now, where were we before we were interrupted?" She giggled, backed away from him, and took another scoop of clotted cream and lobbed it in Noel's direction.

He ducked and then gave her a smile that promised her the world. "Where were we? Oh, yes, food fight, getting naked." He shook the canister.

"Wait! When did this become a food fight? My dress! It will be ruined."

"You started it. As I said, I love how your mind works. And as for your dress, you can always take it off." He took aim.

"Hold on. What about you?"

He paused, setting the whipped cream on the table. "You're right." He tried to unbutton his shirt, gave up, and ripped it open. Buttons bounced to the floor, and then he tore off his shoes and removed his jeans.

"You're taking off all your clothes? What if Mable walks in again?"

"Better lock the door, then."

She rushed to the door and turned the lock as Noel headed straight for her. "Oh, my, you're completely naked. That was fast."

"Can't waste time when a beautiful woman is waiting. Hypothetically, if we were to write more novels together, could we act out the love scenes for our characters?"

She couldn't form a response as erotic thoughts blurred her vision. Her body hummed into overdrive as his hand moved under her dress and up her bare leg. Somehow her dress was unzipped. It slipped over her strapless black bra and barely-there lace panties to pool around her silver stiletto heels. "What about the food fight?"

"Second course." He winked.

She stepped over her dress, moved toward him, and jumped into his arms, straddling his waist. When he lifted her and entered, she gasped. Breathless, she wrapped her arms around his neck and felt his heartbeat in rhythm with hers. "How much time do we have?"

"The rest of our lives."

****

Hours later, Holly awoke beside Noel on Mable's kitchen floor, her head resting in the crook of his arm. She snuggled closer to him. "How did we get on the floor?" She laughed, glancing over at what remained of Mable's table. "Never mind, I remember. We broke her table."

Noel kissed her on the tip of her nose and pulled the lace tablecloth over her shoulders. "I'll build her a new one. You taste like raspberry jam."

She giggled and buried her face with her hands, feeling the heat of a blush blossom and grow. "And you're covered in whipped cream. We'll have to replenish Mable's jam and take showers…"

"Is that an invitation, Miss Lane?"

"It most certainly is, Mr. Atteberry."

She tilted her head toward him and smiled. "It's all rushing back. Time slows when I'm with you." Her eyes widened as she rose on one elbow. "The book signing!"

"You'd fallen asleep when Mable knocked on the door. She said she'd told our readers to return later this evening."

Holly groaned. "Did she say anything about the table?"

He chuckled, kissing her on the shoulder. "Mable called it romantic."

"What else did Mable say?"

"She said, 'It was about time.' "

Holly laughed, sitting up and taking the tablecloth with her. "We should finish the chapter. I know I can write our kiss scene now. All you have to do is the avalanche part."

"About that. There will still be an avalanche, but I've decided that our characters will escape and live happily ever after."

"What changed your mind?"

"You."

A word about the author...

Pam Binder is a *USA Today* and *New York Times* bestselling author who loves Irish and Scottish myths and legends. She is a conference speaker, president of the Pacific Northwest Writers Association, and teaches two year-long novel writing courses, After the First Draft and Write Your Story. Pam writes historical fiction, contemporary fiction, time travel, middle grade, and fantasy.

Visit her at:

http://pambinder.com

Thank you for purchasing
this publication of The Wild Rose Press, Inc.

For questions or more information
contact us at
info@thewildrosepress.com.

The Wild Rose Press, Inc.
www.thewildrosepress.com